"How did you expect me to react?"

Keilly's eyes flashed deep gray as she continued. "Did you expect me to forget everything I know about you? Be flattered that a famous star deigned to kiss me on a deserted beach? Is that what you thought?"

"If it were, I would hardly have bothered to come back," Rod said between clenched teeth. "I wanted you nine weeks ago, and I want you now."

"I won't be your summer affair!"

"There are plenty of women in London who would be only too ready to oblige, if that were all I wanted," he said without conceit. "I want more from you, Keilly."

"I'm not even willing to offer *that* much."

But they both knew that if he pressed for her surrender, she wouldn't be able to refuse him—any more than poor Kathy had been able to refuse him.

Books by Carole Mortimer

HARLEQUIN PRESENTS

443—FIRST LOVE, LAST LOVE
452—SATAN'S MASTER
473—FREEDOM TO LOVE
479—POINT OF NO RETURN
502—ONLY LOVER
510—LOVE'S DUEL
518—BURNING OBSESSION
522—RED ROSE FOR LOVE
531—SHADOWED STRANGER
539—FORGOTTEN LOVER
547—FORBIDDEN SURRENDER
556—ELUSIVE LOVER
564—PASSION FROM THE PAST
571—PERFECT PARTNER
579—GOLDEN FEVER
587—HIDDEN LOVE
594—LOVE'S ONLY DECEPTION
603—CAPTIVE LOVING
611—FANTASY GIRL
619—HEAVEN HERE ON EARTH
627—LIFELONG AFFAIR
636—LOVE UNSPOKEN
645—UNDYING LOVE
651—SUBTLE REVENGE
659—PAGAN ENCHANTMENT
669—TRUST IN SUMMER MADNESS
675—THE FAILED MARRIAGE
684—SENSUAL ENCOUNTER
716—EVERLASTING LOVE
724—HARD TO GET
740—A LOST LOVE
757—UNTAMED

These books may be available at your local bookseller.

CAROLE MORTIMER

untamed

Harlequin Books

TORONTO • NEW YORK • LONDON
AMSTERDAM • PARIS • SYDNEY • HAMBURG
STOCKHOLM • ATHENS • TOKYO • MILAN

For
John and Matthew

Harlequin Presents first edition January 1985
ISBN 0-373-10757-9

Original hardcover edition published in 1984
by Mills & Boon Limited

Printed in U.S.A.

CHAPTER ONE

'MISS KEILLY GRANT, I presume?'

She looked up with a start, used to having the beach to herself this time of the evening, seven o'clock being too late for the children to be here playing, and too early for the late night strollers walking their dogs.

The man standing several feet away from her as she vigorously dried her hair after her swim certainly didn't look as if he fitted into either of those categories. Her first thought was that he was big and powerful, her second that he could be that third category of people that occasionally wandered down to Beachy Cove, the sort of man her Aunt Sylvie was always warning her about—a man looking for an easy pick-up. The cove was usually full of such men during the short summer season, all of them out for a little holiday fun and sure she could provide it. But this man looked too handsome to be that type either, surely having women chasing *him*, not the other way around! Besides, there was the puzzle of him knowing her name.

Nevertheless, she stood up to pull her full-length beach robe over her head, and pulled the zip up to her chin, glad of the warmth of the towelling material after her dip in the coolness of the October sea. The task of covering herself completed, she turned her attention once more to the man standing a short distance away.

He hadn't moved as she dressed, his hands still thrust into the pockets of his thick sheepskin jacket, his shoulders broad and powerful, as was his chest, his legs long and lean in the fitted denims of faded blue, tan-coloured boots on his feet. For all of the casualness of his appearance his clothes looked expensive, and Keilly raised her gaze to his face with more than just idle curiosity. Looking at each feature separately, the piercingly deep blue eyes, the long straight nose, firm but sensual mouth, and strong square jaw, he was nothing spectacular, but put them all together and he was—breathtaking. At least, she assumed his jaw was strong, it was difficult to tell beneath the neatly trimmed beard and moustache, usually finding that such facial hair was grown to hide the weakness of a chin or mouth. In this man's case she doubted that were true; he exuded power and assurance, the deep blue eyes looking at her steadily, as if he didn't allow himself any kind of weakness. His hair was thick and dark, several grey streaks laced through its mahogany colour, although the beard and moustache showed no such ageing. His age was hard to define, perhaps his early thirties, although the lines of experience fanning out from the blue eyes seemed to say he had knowledge far beyond those calendar years.

Keilly took in all this about him in a matter of seconds, knowing he had taken the same few seconds to appraise her own appearance. And she knew it couldn't be very favourable! The salt water had left the feathered style of her shoulder length black hair tangled and lack-lustre, needing the shower she always took after her daily swim to give it back its naturally glossy beauty. Her face was bare of make-up, naturally sooty black lashes framing dark grey eyes that could often look blue, her nose short and stub, her full mouth a deep pink colour, her chin small and determined. It wasn't an unattractive face but neither was it a beautiful one, and her lack of make-up made her appear younger than her twenty-two years. But her body, despite her smallness in stature, was completely adult, full breasts, a slender waist and gently curving hips, her legs long and attractive. And the man in front of her hadn't missed a single inch of her appearance, not before she donned the towelling robe or after, the black bikini showing the tan she still had from the summer months.

She didn't like being made to feel self-conscious about her appearance; as the receptionist in the hotel owned by her aunt and uncle she was usually coolly assured in any situation, had learnt to deal with people with calm patience and understanding. But this man made her feel inadequate in a way she didn't like, her chin rising with stubborn pride. 'Yes, I'm Keilly Grant,' she answered him coolly. 'How did you know who I was?' Because he obviously had known. She had watched his approach as he walked down to the beach from the cliff, and he hadn't even hesitated, coming straight over to her.

His mouth quirked, his teeth very white against the darkness of the surrounding hair. 'Your aunt told me to look for the only lunatic down here swimming,' he looked pointedly at the deserted beach. 'You appear to be it,' he mocked, the blue eyes full of humour.

His voice was deep and attractive, as smooth as honey, filling Keilly with a pleasurable warmth that she dismissed as being ridiculous. She didn't even know who this man was, let alone feel attracted to him! 'My aunt told you where I was,' she said thoughtfully. 'Why were you looking for me in the first place?'

He hunched down even further into his fleecy jacket as a strong October wind blew in from the sea, the fine golden sand about them whipped into the air to land painfully against their faces. 'Could we get off the beach now that you've finished your swim?' The lines had increased about his eyes where he had narrowed them against the wind. 'You're likely to catch pneumonia!'

With a shrug Keilly bent to thrust her wet towel into her beach bag, dangling her shoes from the other hand as they walked across the softness of the sand that led up to the pathway that went to the road on the cliff. 'I only stay in the water a few minutes,' she offered the information stiffly. 'I've swum every day like this since I was a child. And I rarely, if ever, even get a cold,' she announced confidently.

The man at her side glanced back at the grey-black of the Irish Sea, shivering involuntarily. 'It looks freezing!' he grimaced.

'It is,' she gave an amused grin. 'But I can't stand the way it gets so crowded down here during the summer months.'

He quirked dark brows. 'When your aunt and uncle run a hotel?'

'I know,' she pulled a face. 'I should be glad we have the business. But in the summer you can hardly get near the water. *Then* I have to come down at five o'clock in the morning.'

He held her arm as she bent to put on her shoes, maintaining that hold as they began the steep ascent up the cliff path. 'You like to be alone?' he asked softly.

'I don't like to see natural beauty marred by commercialism,' her voice was stilted as she tried to release her arm from his grasp—and was effortlessly restrained from doing so. There was strength in the lean fingers that clasped about her upper arm, a strength she felt sure was tempered so as not to bruise her more delicate flesh. Nevertheless, she didn't like the way he held her, still had no idea who he was or what he was doing here. 'You didn't answer my question,' she turned to look at him, night beginning to fall now. 'Why were you looking for me?'

'I was interested in meeting the woman who wrote so scathingly about Rod Bartlett.'

'Not another reporter!' She gave an exasperated sigh, wrenching her arm away from him to glare up into the deeply tanned face that must have been at least a foot above her in the rapidly falling darkness, this man well over six feet in height, moving with natural grace for such a big man.

'Another one?' he asked curiously, pushing both hands back into his pockets.

Keilly gave him an impatient look. 'Ever since I wrote that letter in reply to a magazine article that was totally egotistical about a man who should be able to earn a living more reputably than by taking his clothes off in a film that had no other purpose than to flaunt his body, I have been inundated with reporters trying to find out what my angle is.' Her mouth twisted with distaste. 'Most of them seem to think I'm a scorned lover.'

'And are you?'

The quietly voiced question had the effect of making her anger flare higher than ever. 'No, I am not!' she snapped furiously.

'Then what *is* your angle?'

Her eyes flashed a warning. 'Just who are you?'

'Another reporter, I'm afraid,' he revealed with regret. 'Rick Richards,' he held out his hand to her.

Keilly ignored it, not even breathing hard from the exertion as they reached the level of the road, although it irked her to see that neither was Rick Richards, obviously a man who kept himself in condition. She could feel grudging respect for that, even if she heartily disliked his profession.

His hand dropped back to his side as he once again fell into step beside her. 'Nice to meet you too,' he derided softly.

She didn't answer, just wanting to shake him off as she had the other reporters, wishing now that she had never given in to the impulse to write that scathing letter to the widely circulated magazine. It was just that it made her blood boil when she read what a brilliant actor Rod Bartlett was, how good looking, how macho, when she knew what sort of man he really was. He was egotistical, completely selfish, giving no thought to anyone but himself and furthering his career. His three year, much-publicised, affair with a woman ten years his senior several years ago was proof of that. Until he became Veronica King's lover he had been virtually unknown; after moving in with her he had suddenly made meteoric stardom. And he hadn't cared who he trod on or who he hurt to get there. He would be thirty years of age now, had been much in demand for almost ten years—and Keilly couldn't even bring herself to go and see even one of the twenty or so films he had made during that time. She just wasn't interested in Rod Bartlett and how wonderful everyone thought he was, his female fans going wild when it was revealed that in his latest film he actually appeared naked for several minutes. The film was still doing the rounds of the cinemas six months after its release, was reputedly breaking box-office records.

'My refusal to speak about the matter is not a personal insult to you, Mr Richards——'

'Rick,' he put in with that smoothly charming voice. 'I prefer Rick.'

She shot him an irritated glance. 'Well, my refusal to talk about Rod Bartlett is simply because I don't have any more to say on the subject.'

'Probably not,' he gave a throaty chuckle. 'You were pretty vocal in your letter. Now what was it you said about the fact that Rod Bartlett hasn't returned to this,

his home-town, for almost twelve years? Ah yes,' his mouth twisted with humour. ' "Perhaps Mr Bartlett is too ashamed to show his face here—or any other part of his anatomy that cinema-goers are now so familiar with." I think I have that more or less right, don't I?' he mused.

Hot colour had stained her cheeks at his word-perfect quote from her letter. She had written it with searing contempt, little dreaming it would cause such a stir. The first reporter to come here and try to interview her had come from the magazine itself, and after her had come a steady stream of them, all looking for some as-yet undiscovered scandal in Rod Bartlett's past. Keilly hadn't been about to tell them anything, and she didn't intend Rick Richards to be any different. She just wanted to forget she had ever written the damned letter.

'But not you, Keilly?'

'Not me what?' she frowned at the question, not understanding it.

'You aren't familiar with the anatomy of Rod Bartlett?'

'How dare you!' she flared indignantly. 'I've never even met the man!'

'I meant up on the big screen,' he mocked.

Her mouth twisted with derision. 'I have no wish to see Rod Bartlett up on the "big screen" or anywhere else. He just doesn't interest me.'

Rick nodded. 'But why did you use the word ashamed? Does he have a wife and ten kids hidden down here somewhere?' he mocked.

'Don't be ridiculous!' she snapped.

'Then what is the big secret?'

'There isn't one!' she almost shouted her exasperation. 'I just don't happen to agree with the general consensus that Rod Bartlett has the sex appeal of Rudolph

Valentino, the good looks of Paul Newman, Steve McQueen, and Robert Redford all rolled into one dynamic package! I'm entitled to my opinion, Mr Richards.'

He held up his hands defensively. 'I'm not disputing that. It just seemed to me, and obviously to others too, that it was a very personal attack. Too personal in some ways.'

Once again the colour darkened her cheeks, and she was relieved to see they were nearing the hotel where she lived with her aunt and uncle. 'I told you, Mr— Rick,' she amended at his raised brows. 'I've never met the man.'

'No,' he gave her a considering look. 'You look a little young for him.'

She bristled resentfully. 'He prefers *older* women, I understand.'

'You mean Veronica King?' the man at her side voice softly, his expression unreadable in the gloom of dusk.

'Of course,' she said dismissively. 'Everyone conveniently forgets, six years later, that the two of them lived together, that the poor woman was so devastated by the rumours of his other women that she crashed her plane and killed herself rather than go through the humiliation of losing him to someone who could give him more than she could.'

'You seem so certain that's the way it happened?'

'The newspapers were sure too at the time!'

'The same newspapers you now think exaggerate everything about the man?'

She gave Rick a look of intense dislike, hating the way he twisted her words to confuse her. She *knew* how selfish Rod Bartlett was, she didn't need the newspapers to tell her anything about him. 'I have to go in and shower, Mr Richards,' she told him distantly. 'If you'll excuse me. . . .' His hand on her arm stopped her going into the cheery warmth of the hotel that had become her home on the death of her mother fifteen years ago, her aunt and uncle taking her into their family without a qualm, their daughter, her senior by six years, becoming the elder sister she never had.

'Have dinner with me,' he invited huskily.

Her eyes darkened with confusion. 'I always eat with my aunt and uncle,' she refused.

'Couldn't you make tonight the exception?'

She felt almost as if she were drowning in the sensuous warmth of liquid blue eyes, held mesmerised by him as he compelled her to accept. 'I—I suppose I could,' she heard herself say. 'As long as you don't intend to talk about Rod Bartlett all evening,' she warned firmly.

He grinned, suddenly looking younger. 'I promise you I won't quote a single word you say about him.'

'You do?' she blinked, strangely believing him when she hadn't trusted any of the other reporters who had pestered her.

'I do,' he nodded. 'Now do you want to eat here at the hotel or do you know of any good restaurants nearby?'

Keilly's eyes widened. 'You're staying here?'

'Of course,' he sounded mockingly scandalised. 'You don't think your aunt would give your whereabouts to just anyone, do you?' He smiled, looking rakishly attractive, a little like the pirates must have done long ago, the beard and moustache suiting him.

She brought her thoughts up sharp as she caught herself wondering what it was like to kiss a man with a beard. She had agreed to have dinner with the man, nothing else. Although in the circumstances it might be better if they ate right here at the hotel.

'Coward,' Rick murmured after she told him her decision, bending so close his breath warmed her ear. 'And I've been told on good authority that it doesn't tickle at all,' he murmured throatily.

She moved jerkily away from him, almost as if she had been burnt, looking up at him with wide eyes.

'They're very expressive,' gentle fingertips moved across her lids, 'I can almost read every thought you have.'

'As long as it remains only almost,' she said waspishly. 'I'll meet you in the dining room in an hour—er—Rick.'

'I'll be waiting, Keilly,' he added softly, watching until she disappeared through a door behind the main desk marked 'Private'.

Keilly felt his gaze on her the whole time, wondering if she hadn't perhaps been a little impetuous in agreeing to have dinner with him; she had treated the other reporters with a bluntness that bordered on rudeness. It wasn't even as if she knew anything about Rick, only his name, that he was staying at the hotel, and that he was interested in her dislike of Rod Bartlett. It was the latter part that bothered her. All reporters seemed to have an inborn natural curiosity, a need to probe until they unearthed what they were looking for. And if Rick Richards did that this time he would be hurting a lot of people. Damn the flash of temper that had given her the courage to write that scathing letter and so draw attention to herself and Selchurch!

She erased the dark frown from her brow as she went through to the kitchen to see her aunt, kissing her affectionately. 'Dinner smells good,' she greeted warmly, the aroma of food being cooked filling the room.

Her aunt smiled, small and plump, enjoying running the relatively big hotel in this small northern sea-side town, having built up a steady clientele the last twenty-five years. 'Did Mr Richards manage to find you?'

Keilly's gaze was suddenly evasive, not wanting to disclose that he was yet another reporter looking for a story. They had been plagued with them this last month, and she knew it worried her aunt. 'Yes, he found me,' she acknowledged lightly. 'I'm going to have dinner with him, in fact,' she added brightly.

'Here?'

'That's right,' she nodded. 'I'm going to be a guest for a change,' she teased.

Her Aunt Sylvie joined in her humour, although she still looked a little puzzled. 'Is he a friend of yours? I don't remember you ever mentioning him.'

For a brief moment she toyed with the idea of agreeing he was a friend, and then she dismissed the idea. She would need Rick Richards' cooperation for such a ploy, and she had no reason to suppose he would give it. 'He's another reporter,' she admitted with a sigh.

'Oh dear,' her aunt gave a rueful grimace. 'And he seemed such a nice young man too.'

The thought of Rick ever being thought 'a nice young man' was amusing enough in itself, but the fact that her aunt thought his profession precluded him ever being such was hilarious. Keilly began to giggle, finally laughing outright.

'What is it, dear?' her aunt looked troubled.

She contained her humour with effort. 'Being a reporter isn't like having a contagious disease, Aunt Sylvie. The poor man can't help his profession.'

Her aunt still looked disapproving. 'One or two of them that came down here could have done with better manners,' she reproved. 'And some of the questions they asked your Uncle Bill and I,' she looked scandalised. 'I'm sure they expected you to have that actor's baby at least!'

'Aunt Sylvie!' she gasped, not having realised just how personal the reporters had become with her family.

Her aunt shrugged. 'That's what several of them implied. I hope Mr Richards isn't going to be as offensive,' she frowned.

Keilly shook her head. 'I've already told him I've never met Rod Bartlett. I'm sure he believed me.' She picked up her beach bag. 'I'd better go and wash the salt and sand off me.'

'See you later, darling,' her aunt returned to her cooking.

Keilly knew exactly what sort of scandalous story the reporters had expected to find here, but she hadn't realised any of them had gone so far as to burden her aunt and uncle with such questions. She intended telling Rick Richards exactly enough to get him to leave Selchurch and no more. She had no more than that to tell him anyway.

He was waiting in the bar when she came downstairs an hour later, not noticing her at first as he chatted easily with her uncle as he stood behind the bar, Rick relaxing on one of the bar stools. The sheepskin jacket had gone now, a brown jacket and cream shirt in its place, showing her that she had been right about his shoulders and chest; he was powerfully muscled. The tailored trousers were the same cream colour as his partly unbuttoned shirt, their style and cut drawing provocative attention to the muscular leanness of his legs and thighs. He looked as if he too had showered during the last hour, the short neatly styled hair still damp.

Her uncle said something to make him laugh before moving off to serve some local people who had just come into the bar. Rick turned slightly away, his eyes widening as he saw Keilly standing in the doorway, warming to a deep blue as he took in her appearance, making her feel pleased that she had taken so much trouble with her hair and dress. She couldn't ever remember feeling so warmed by a man's open appreciation before.

Her hair was darkly gleaming now, blow-dried into its feathered windswept style to her shoulders, her make-up light and subtle, blue shading over dark grey eyes, her high cheekbones darkened by blusher, her lip-gloss of burnt orange. Her dress was knee-length, black shot through with silver weave, a black sash belt tied about her narrow waist, black high-heeled sandals adding to her elegance.

She could see her efforts had all been worth it as Rick stood up to slowly come towards her. 'I hardly recognised you,' he admitted huskily, standing only inches away now. 'And I mean that in the nicest possible way.'

Keilly eyed him shyly, slightly unnerved by his own appearance. He was certainly nothing like the usual sort of man they had staying here, the hotel catering mainly for families. It was a long time since she had been in the company of such an attractive man, and now she felt rather awkward, wishing once again that she hadn't agreed to have dinner with him.

He seemed to sense she was almost ready to take flight, lightly clasping her arm, his hand almost seeming to burn where it touched. 'Shall we go through to the dining room?'

'Your drink?' her voice came out huskily.

He shrugged dismissal of it. 'We can have some wine

with our meal,' he decided arrogantly.

Keilly allowed herself to be led into the intimacy of the small dining room they used during the winter months, smiling at the young waitress as she came to take their order, her smile fading slightly as she saw the appreciative look Brenda was giving Rick.

He looked at the small but extensive menu. 'What do you recommend?' he seemed completely unaware of the other girl's interest in him.

It was a dangerous quality, the ability he had to make the woman he was with feel as if she were the only person important to him, and Keilly's voice was unnaturally sharp because of it. 'Everything,' she told him abruptly. 'My aunt does all the cooking, and she's good.'

They both ordered the duck, Rick looking at the other empty tables. 'Not very busy tonight,' he remarked softly.

She shrugged. 'It's out of season, we're never busy in October. In fact, you're our only guest at the moment. Although we do serve meals to anyone who cares to come in.' She looked pointedly at the empty room. 'The people of Selchurch prefer to eat at home in the winter as a rule.' She picked up the glass of vodka and lime he had ordered for her, sipping it slowly, looking anywhere but at the compelling man sitting across the table from her. 'How long are you staying?' she asked casually.

'This time?' He sat back in his chair, totally relaxed. 'Just tonight. But I may come back,' he added throatily, his dark gaze intent on the beauty of her face, forcing her to look at him with the insistence that she should.

He was flirting with her, she knew that, with his words but without actually touching her. He didn't need to touch her, just the warmth of his gaze was like a caress. But he *was* only here for the one night, and despite what he said to the contrary she doubted he would ever come back here. With his cool sophistication he was more suited to London than this small northern town, and once he got back there he would forget all about Keilly Grant, the woman who had caused a minor stir because she dared to criticise Rod Bartlett, the darling of the film world.

She waited for their meal to be served before speaking again, her voice waspish as she saw the smile he bestowed on the already besotted Brenda. 'Which newspaper do you work for?'

'Which——? Oh I'm freelance,' he replied easily. 'I write an article and then try and sell it,' he added by way of explanation.

'Whatever takes the public's interest,' she derided.

'Which at the moment is you,' Rick drawled. 'You've caused quite a sensation, little lady.'

Her mouth twisted. 'Because I don't happen to think Rod Bartlett is wonderful!' her tone showed her contempt for such a thing being important.

Rick shook his head. 'Because you came out and said it.'

'Isn't that allowed?' she taunted.

'Apparently not,' he mused, sipping the wine that had been poured for them, consulting her on his choice, not one of those men who arrogantly assumed they knew the likes and dislikes of the person they were dining with and ordered for them. Keilly couldn't stand such dominating men, and although Rick appeared to be forceful he certainly wasn't inconsiderate. 'Yours was the only letter of dissension they received at the magazine about the article. You should have seen the sacks of mail they received from people who wanted to lynch you from the nearest tree once your letter had been published,' he derided.

'All of them women,' Keilly dismissed scornfully.

'Actually, no,' he refuted gently. 'Rod Bartlett has quite a following among both sexes.'

'Men wishing they were as macho as him,' her mouth twisted with distaste.

Rick narrowed puzzled blue eyes. 'He really did do something to upset you, didn't he.'

She flushed. 'Don't tell me you think he's wonderful too!'

He seemed to hestitate, an emotion that didn't sit well on such a decisive man. 'Have you seen "Beginning Again"?' he named Rod Bartlett's most recent film.

'Certainly not,' she snapped. 'But you obviously have,' she looked at him accusingly.

'It's a beautiful and sensitive film——'

'Nothing about Rod Bartlett could possibly be beautiful or sensitive,' she cut in heatedly, and then wished she hadn't as he gave her yet another speculative look. She had to remember that no matter how charming and easy to talk to Rick was he was still a reporter, and reporters had been known to forget all ethics if they thought they were on the trail of a story. Rick had only promised not to quote her, not to refrain from writing the story altogether. 'There's no room for nakedness in a beautiful and sensitive film,' she added uncomfortably.

'How do you know that if you haven't seen it?'

She flushed at his quiet rebuke, the food on her plate only half eaten as Brenda took them back to the kitchen, although Rick seemed to be experiencing no such loss of appetite, eating all of his food. 'I thought you said we wouldn't talk about Rod Bartlett all evening,' she reminded waspishly.

'And I don't intend to,' there was a dark promise in his steady gaze. 'Not all evening. But I wondered what your reaction was to him coming back here?'

Keilly raised a stricken gaze to him, sure she couldn't have heard him correctly. 'I—Did you say he was coming to Selchurch?' she swallowed hard.

'It's been rumoured that he is,' Rick nodded. 'I have a friend on the magazine you wrote to—Jeanie. I think you met her?'

She nodded, remembering the tall blonde woman who had arrived from the magazine to interview her. She wondered how much of a 'friend' the beautiful woman was to Rick, and then chastised herself for these ridiculous feelings of jealousy. After tonight she would never seen him again, and one casual dinner together certainly didn't give her the right to be jealous of the other women in his life.

'She's the one who interviewed Bartlett for the article,' Rick continued softly. 'Apparently he mentioned that he's taking a break soon. He hasn't stopped working for the last five years, you know.'

'I'm sure he hasn't,' Keilly derided. 'But that hasn't prevented him *playing* either.'

Rick shrugged. 'A man needs relaxation of some kind——'

'So does a woman,' she bit out.

'Then no one gets hurt, do they,' he shrugged.

Keilly gave him a disbelieving look. 'Is that what you really believe?' she asked slowly.

'Keilly——'

'Do you?' she insisted he answer, impatient with his reasoning tone.

He sighed, the blue eyes hard now. 'If a man and woman want to sleep together, for whatever reason, mutual gratification, love, then surely that is their business and no one else's?'

'And if only one of them loves?' Her eyes flashed deeply grey, neither of them making any effort to eat the dessert that had been placed in front of them minutes earlier.

His mouth firmed impatiently. 'Keilly——'

She moved her hand from the table down on to her knee as he would have grasped it. 'You were telling me about Rod Bartlett coming back here,' she prompted stiffly.

Rick shrugged dismissal of the subject, looking at her exasperatedly. 'He mentioned to Jeanie that he was thinking about it.'

'When?'

'He was only thinking about it, Keilly,' he sighed.

'He'll probably decide to go to the Bahamas instead,' she scorned.

Rick shook his head. 'He isn't that keen on hot weather,' his mouth twisted at the wind that could now be heard blowing in strongly from the sea. 'This would suit him a lot better.'

'He won't find any bikini-clad beauties down here!'

He smiled. 'He'll find one,' he teased. 'And very beautiful she is too.'

Keilly blushed at this blatant flirtation, although her thoughts were far from the man seated opposite her. It would be disastrous for the actor to come to Selchurch! Perhaps it had just been a whim, one he had instantly dismissed? After all, he hadn't been back for twelve years, so why should he decide to come back now? It had probably just been talk, people like him were always trying to convince the public that they hadn't forgotten their 'roots'. Nevertheless, her unease about the idea persisted. If he *should* come back——

'Why do I get the feeling I'm rather superfluous?' Rick drawled self-derisively.

He looked quite put out by the fact that she kept fading off into her thoughts and ignoring him. And she could understand why. He was too attractive, too attentive a companion himself to usually be treated in this off-hand manner.

She gave a light laugh, forgetting the actor for the moment, forgetting the chaos he could cause if he did decide to come back here even if only for a visit, concentrating on the man she was with, intent on enjoying what little time she had left with him. He would be gone in the morning and she would never see him again. 'You aren't superfluous at all,' she told him throatily, looking at him beneath lowered lashes. 'Not as far as I'm concerned anyway.' She sat back as the waitress removed their used dishes. 'Or Brenda either,' she added as the other girl gave him yet another yearning look. 'We don't get many attractive men staying here and——' she broke off as she realised what she had said, then cursed herself for blushing like a schoolgirl.

Rick's eyes brimmed with laughter. 'Please go on,' he drawled softly. 'You had got as far as "attractive man" . . .'

'*Men*,' she corrected, sighing as she couldn't contain her own humour any longer, meeting the smile in his eyes. 'You haven't reached thirty, thirty-two——'

'Thirty-one,' he supplied.

'Well you haven't reached that age without being aware of your own attraction,' she dismissed. 'Or how women react to it.' She was amazed at herself; she didn't usually indulge in such openly flirtatious conversations with virtual strangers, in fact she didn't have conversations like this at all normally. Rick seemed to dispense with all inhibitions, demanding and receiving honesty.

He leant forward now, taking one of her hands as she plucked nervously at the tablecloth, his thumb moving erotically against her palm. 'How do you react to it?'

She felt uncomfortable under his probing gaze, her hand tingling where he touched her, sending messages of pleasure up through her body. 'The same way Brenda does,' she admitted huskily. 'I just hide it better,' she added dryly.

Rick continued to look at her for long timeless minutes. 'Come for a walk with me,' he requested suddenly.

She gave him a startled glance. 'It sounds as if its blowing a gale out there.' The wind could clearly be heard howling around the building, seeming to grow stronger by the minute.

'It's untamed, like you,' he told her intently, standing up, her hand still held firmly in his as he pulled her towards him. 'When I saw you on the beach tonight I could see you belonged here——'

'I was born here——'

'I didn't mean that,' Rick dismissed shortly. 'You belong *here*, in this environment, with the sea and the wind as your friends.' His hand came up to frame her face as he held her gaze up to his. 'Your eyes remind me of the sea on a day like this,' he murmured softly, seeming to devour her as he sought to commit the mental image of her to memory. 'They're deep and dark, deep enough for a man to lose his soul in.'

'Rick——' She broke apart from him as the kitchen door swung open behind them, Brenda coming to a self-conscious halt as she saw them standing so closely together. Keilly blushed a dark red, knowing it would be all over the town tomorrow that she had been seen kissing one of the guests in the dining room. The fact that she and Rick hadn't actually been kissing each other was irrelevent, all three of them knew that if Brenda had come in a few seconds later they would have been. 'We've finished now, thank you, Brenda,' her voice was sharp before she turned to leave the room knowing, but not seeing, that Rick was at her side as she did so.

'I'm sorry,' he said softly after several silent seconds.

She came to a halt in the reception area, turning to look at him. 'For what?'

He shrugged. 'The dining room of your aunt and uncle's hotel isn't the place for me to attempt to seduce you,' he derided. 'I'm sorry if I embarrassed you.'

'You didn't,' she returned abruptly. 'Thank you for dinner, Mr Richards,' she held out her hand politely. 'I hope you've enjoyed your stay here with us.'

He looked down at the hand she held out to him, ignoring the fact that she expected him to shake it, taking it firmly in his left hand to pull her against his side. 'I believe I suggested we go for a walk,' he reminded throatily.

'It's cold and windy——'

'You love it like this,' he dismissed. 'In fact, I bet you revel in it. I can just picture you now, walking along the beach on starlit nights, defying the elements, the sea.'

Keilly stared up at him in surprised wonder. No one else had ever realised the challenge she found in a night like this, the battle she had with the sea each time she swam in the winter evenings. The rest of the family and her friends just thought she was a 'health nut', none of them had ever realised how she really felt about it. Rick had only known her a couple of hours, and yet he had guessed, he *knew*.

'I'll go and get my coat,' she told him quietly.

He nodded, pleasure flaring in his eyes to make them appear sapphire blue. 'And I'll get mine.'

He was waiting outside for her when she came through from collecting her thick woollen coat, pulling the tie-belt tightly about her waist as she looked up and met his gaze. During their few minutes apart she hadn't liked to allow herself the time to think, hadn't wanted to, for once just wanted to enjoy the moment, of being with someone who knew her so totally. He held out his arms to her now and she didn't hesitate about moving into them, her head bent back as she raised her mouth for his kiss, receiving no gentle exploration to her trusting gesture, swept away on a tide of passion so strong it equalled the force of the wind that whipped her hair about their faces, touching the hardness of Rick's cheeks as if in a caress.

They didn't speak as they drew apart, turning as if by tacit agreement to walk towards the cove, Keilly snuggled against the warmth of his coat as his arm remained possessively about her shoulders.

She felt warmed, protected, braving a glance at the enigmatic man who made her feel that way. He walked strong and proud, his head into the wind, as if he too enjoyed challenging the elements—although unlike her, he seemed confident he could win!

'You're right,' she broke the silence between them as they stood at the top of the cliff looking down, the white surf of the wind-tossed sea crashing against the sand. 'It doesn't tickle,' she added almost shyly, his facial hair feeling softer than she had imagined, not rough at all.

Rick smiled at her with complete accord, moving off again, taking her down the moonlit pathway to the beach below. It wasn't windy against the cliffs in the shelter of the cove, a strange stillness all around them.

Once again Keilly felt compelled to raise her face to him, her lips parted to the sensual assault of his, her arms clasped about his neck as she stood on tiptoe, held fast against him by the strong arms he wrapped so possessively about her slender body.

She felt herself lowered lightly to stand on the ground as his mouth travelled across her cheek to her throat, her arms against his shirt beneath his jacket, her head thrown back as he released the top two buttons to her dress, exposing the curve of her breasts beneath the black lacy bra, his lips moving across their exposed fullness before capturing hers once again.

This time he kissed her deeply, intimately, the smoothness of his tongue entering her mouth to run lightly along the edge of her inner lips, plunging deeper as she groaned her surrender, the tautness of his thighs so hard against hers heady to her already aroused senses.

'We can't make love here!' he groaned as he bit into her earlobe, tracing the gentle curve with his tongue.

'No,' she agreed, his chest bared to her questing hands and lips.

'The sand is probably as damp as hell,' he muttered between fevered kisses on her bared shoulders.

'Yes,' she said again, gasping slightly as he bit into her tender flesh, hearing his groan of satisfaction seconds later as her tongue sought and found the male nipple, feeling it harden beneath her caresses.

With the minimum of movement he had thrown off his sheepskin jacket and was lowering her down on to it, smoothing aside the unbuttoned front of her dress, releasing the fastening of her bra to bare her breasts to his avid gaze.

The sky could have fallen in on them at that moment and neither of them would have cared, Keilly arching up as his mouth claimed moist possession of one rosy-tipped breast, teeth closing about the nipple to bite down gently as ecstasy flooded her lower limbs, a slow warmth invading her thighs, the pleasure ten-fold as his hand claimed the other breast, his thumb moving roughly across the tip.

Both were oblivious to the storm rolling in off the sea, lost in a tempest of their own making, moist lips claiming other welcoming lips, hands avidly searching the pleasure spots of their bodies.

Rick's hand was on her knee now, travelling slowly up her thigh, closing possessively over the delicious mound that lay beneath black lacy panties, the warmth increasing in Keilly as he slowly caressed her there, his hand moving surely beneath the lace to the waiting flesh below.

The storm of their making may have been strong, but the storm above them wasn't to be denied any longer, huge drops of rain falling coldly on their heated flesh, Rick's shirt soaked and clinging to his back within seconds as he lay across her. Even so he was loath to relinquish her mouth, leaving her with a frustrated groan, quickly buttoning her dress for her before pulling her coat warmly about her.

'Your coat——'

'I'll see to that in a minute,' he dismissed, his hair looking as black as her own now that it was wet. 'Keilly,' his hands framed her face, seemingly oblivious to the rain that was fast drenching them both. 'No matter how much I wanted you just now I wouldn't have taken you here,' his gaze held hers steadily. 'Making love on a beach, fumbling about in the dark as if we're guilty of something, it isn't how I want our first time together to be.' His head bent and he kissed her slowly, lingeringly. 'I'm going to give you champagne and roses when I make love to you. And a bed,' he added meaningly.

She was warmed by the sincerity of his words, knew that the rain, the frantic haste to straighten their clothes, had dampened things in more ways than one. Rick taking the time—and getting waterlogged into the bargain!—to reassure her of his feelings made everything seem good again.

'A bed can be made of many things, Rick,' she sat up to assist him with his coat, although it was much too late to prevent him being soaked to the skin. 'Down or sand, the important thing is who you share it with.'

He smiled, his eyes a deep warm blue. 'My untamed witch!' He bent to kiss her with lingering tenderness, his gaze intent for long breathless seconds before he quickly stood up, pulling her lightly to her feet. 'Are there any caves along here where we can wait until the rain stops?' He narrowed his eyes along the cliff face.

'No caves,' she took his hand and began to run. 'But there's an overhanging rock where we can take shelter.'

They reached the rock within minutes, huddling close together to avoid the worst of the rain.

As they stood there waiting for the onslaught to ease, reaction began to set in for Keilly. It was inevitable that it should, in all of her twenty-two years she could never remember behaving this wantonly before, and with a virtual stranger. She had been out with quite a few men, and several of them would have liked the relationship to progress further than the goodnight kisses she allowed them, but always in the past she had held out, knowing that most of them were just out for another conquest, someone they could tell their friends about afterwards.

But Rick was much older than any of the other men she had dated, was surely past the stage in his life where he needed to boast about physical conquests in order to feel good. And she believed him when he said he hadn't intended making love to her on the beach, knew that no matter how aroused he had been he had also been completely in control, that he had had no intention of making their lovemaking into something childish and illicit.

'I won't come to your room tonight,' she murmured against the dampness of his coat.

'I know that.'

'And you aren't coming to mine either!'

'No. Keilly,' he raised her face gently with his hand. 'I told you, I'm coming back. And I meant it.'

Happiness glowed in the darkness of her eyes. 'When?'

'I'm not sure yet—I *will* be back, Keilly,' he insisted as disappointment clouded her face. 'Now that I've found you I'll let no other man tame you but me!' His arms tightened painfully. 'All that wildness and fire is going to be for me,' he ground out fiercely.

She didn't know if she were relieved or disappointed when it at last stopped raining ten minutes later, relieved because they could at last go and get out of these wet clothes, disappointed because she didn't want this time with Rick to end.

He seemed to share her reluctance, for all that they were both wet and cold their walk back to the hotel was slow, their arms wrapped about each other hindering their speed even more. And neither of them minded in the least, stopping outside the hotel to kiss once more.

'I was going to organise a search-party,' her uncle Bill sighed his relief as they entered the hotel, a small wiry man with sandy-grey hair and twinkling blue eyes. 'You had better go upstairs and shower, Keilly, before you catch pneumonia.'

'She doesn't even catch cold,' Rick murmured, his gaze still locked on her flushed cheeks.

'That's true,' her uncle nodded. 'By the way, there was a telephone call for you while you were out, Mr Richards.'

Keilly felt the way Rick suddenly stiffened with tension, looking up at him enquiringly.

'For me?' he frowned. 'Are you sure?'

Her uncle smiled. 'Well you are our only guest, and the lady was quite clear about the name. She left a message for you here somewhere,' he looked through the papers on the desk. '"Call Barbie",' he read. 'Urgent, she said it was,' he frowned.

'Thanks,' Rick nodded abstractedly. 'I'll call her as soon as I've changed.'

Keily could still sense his tension as he held on tightly to her hand. 'Anything wrong, Rick?' she prompted softly.

'No,' he shook his head. 'Barbie—sometimes finds work for me,' he explained abruptly. 'We had both better do as your uncle suggested and take a shower.'

'Separately, I hope,' her Uncle Bill put in dryly.

Keilly's indignant gasp was drowned out by the men's shared laughter, and with a fierce glare at both of them she walked off to take her shower—alone! Really, she couldn't imagine what had come over her uncle for him to make such a personal remark.

One look in the mirror once she reached her bedroom on the top floor showed her exactly why he had done it. Despite the wet slickness of her hair, slightly smudged make-up, and limp clothing, it was possible to see she had been thoroughly kissed, and by an expert too if the glow in her eyes was anything to go by.

'Keilly?' A knock sounded on the door to accompany the soft calling of her name. 'Keilly, I have to talk to you.'

Rick! 'I meant what I said earlier,' she spoke to him through the thickness of the door.

'I know, darling,' he sounded amused. 'But I have to return to London tonight, and I——'

'Tonight?' she had the door open before he could even finish what he was saying. 'Tonight, Rick?' she groaned her disappointment, uncaring that she was revealing too much of her feelings; she had thought they had until tomorrow morning at least.

He was still as wet as she was, although his shorter hair was drying quicker than hers. 'I decided to call Barbie right away, and—I have a job to do back in London,' he shrugged. 'I'll be leaving as soon as I've changed and packed.'

She couldn't even manage a smile. 'Barbie is—just a friend?'

He smiled gently, pulling her into his arms. 'Just a friend—my little witch.' He sobered suddenly. 'I don't want to go now, but I have to. You do believe I'll come back?'

At the moment she wanted to believe anything he told her, nodding before she found her mouth claimed by his, kissing him back as if she never wanted him to stop.

They were both breathing hard by the time they pulled apart, Rick resting his forehead momentarily on hers before moving away from her completely. 'I'd better go—or I won't want to,' he added ruefully. 'I'll call you, okay?' He touched her cheek with gentle fingertips.

She swallowed hard. 'Okay.'

With one last rakish grin he was gone, leaving Keilly wondering if she had imagined it all, if Rick Richards had just been a wonderful dream. But the tingle all over her body told her he couldn't have been, and when she undressed the slight redness to her breasts where his beard had scraped her more tender skin more than convinced her that he had been real.

But would he really come back or had she just been

an interlude to him? Worse still, would she find a story about herself emblazoned across some newspaper in the next few days, Rick Richards' personal—*very* personal, interview with the woman who had scorned at Rod Bartlett?

Oh God, Rod Bartlett! She had forgotten about him the last couple of hours. There was a possibility—even if only a very remote one—that Rod Bartlett could come back here. How was Kathy going to react to that?

CHAPTER TWO

'I'LL have to leave town! I'll have to emigrate,' her cousin and closest friend groaned. 'Oh, Keilly, what *shall* I do?' she wailed.

She didn't have an answer for her, felt too awful herself to be able to tackle anyone else's problems, even Kathy's. In payment for her over-confidence about how healthy she was she had been in bed with the flu the last two days since Rick's departure! She had woken the following morning with a throat that felt like sandpaper, and a head that ached so much it felt as if it were about to split open, the coughing and sneezing coming later, along with the hot flushes and cold chills.

Kathy had called to see her this afternoon, although Keilly still felt far from up to seeing visitors, but knowing she would have to tell her cousin about Rod Bartlett's proposed visit. As she had known she would be, Kathy was almost hysterical at the thought of it.

'He may not come,' she blew her nose noisily, armed with her second box of tissues in as many days, her nose a bright unattractive red. 'Rick only said it was a possibility.'

Kathy still looked worried, her beautiful face marred by the deep frown to her brow. Her hair was the colour of golden sunlight, long and glowing just past her shoulders, her figure tall and willowy, her choice of clothes always impeccable, the cream tailored suit and rust coloured blouse with its tied-bow neckline suiting her perfectly, making the brown of her eyes look like deep sherry. Kathy was as beautiful inside as she was out, and Keilly had loved her as a sister from the moment she had come to live here. She wished there was something she could do to help her cousin now, but there wasn't.

'Did this Rick talk as if he really knew?' Kathy chewed on her bottom lip, uncaring that she removed the dark orange lip-gloss in the process.

She shrugged. 'He seemed to have contacts in the right places.' She had kept her mind clear of thoughts of Rick, not allowing herself to even think about him and the way she had behaved with him on the beach. She hadn't expected him to telephone her immediately he got to London, but this was the third day after his departure and still he hadn't called. But at least she had been reassured by the fact that no story appeared about her in the newspapers. If that could be reassuring. She still doubted that she would ever see him again—and that was what she didn't want to think of. 'And he knew the woman who did the original Rod Bartlett interview.' She had no doubt that Rick knew a lot of women, with his easy charm and ability to make the woman he happened to be with feel like someone special in his life he was sure to!

She had thought a lot of her own response to him, and she was no nearer to fully understanding her reaction to him. Oh she knew her fiery response had been the result of an experienced lover, she just didn't understand why it had happened with Rick, a complete stranger until that night. Other men she had been out with in the past had shown the same physical experience, but always with them she had been able to say no. Her refusal not to let their relationship go any further had only been a gesture on her part, they both knew he had been the one to decide they shouldn't make love. That was what worried her. She wanted

Rick to come back, and yet she feared what might happen if he did, feared her own fate could be that of her mother's.

Kathy gave a worried sigh. 'What will I do if Rod does come back here?' she frowned. 'How will I face him?'

Her eyes widened indignantly. 'I would have thought it would be the other way round,' she said archly. 'He was the one who seduced you, remember?'

'Well of course,' her cousin dismissed shortly. 'But that doesn't make it any less embarrassing for me.'

Keilly could understand that, could still remember Kathy's distress on her wedding morning six years ago. She had been her cousin's only bridesmaid, had been helping Kathy get out the snowy white dress she was to wear that afternoon when the other girl had suddenly burst into tears.

'It's no good,' she cried. 'I can't go through with it.'

Keilly had held her consolingly, smiling her understanding with this sudden attack of nerves. 'It's all right, love,' she soothed. 'All brides feel like this.'

'No, they don't,' Kathy wailed. 'Oh God, I wish I were dead!'

'Kathy!'

'Well I do,' her cousin stood up to move restlessly about the room, 'I love Peter so much, and I—I have no right to marry him.'

'Of course you do——'

'No, I don't,' Kathy shook her head, her hands clenched tightly in front of her. 'I have no right to wear white today either.'

Sixteen-year-old Keilly had frowned her puzzlement. 'What do you mean?'

'You can't be that innocent!' Kathy snapped. 'It's usually only virgins that wear white, so it must be obvious that I'm not one!'

Keilly stared at her in stunned disbelief. The two girls had been the best of friends for the last nine years, had confided everything in each other, and never once had Kathy said anything like this before. 'You and Peter——'

'No, not *Peter* and me,' her cousin groaned her unhappiness. 'Do you think I would be in this state if it were Peter who had been my lover?'

Keilly paled. 'Someone else . . .?'

'Yes,' Kathy sat down heavily.

She swallowed hard, finding it difficult to take all this in. 'But you and Peter have been going out together for years, when could you have— When you were at college in London!' she suddenly realised. 'Is that when it happened, Kathy?'

'*Yes*,' her cousin groaned, her eyes shadowed with pain. 'He was so good looking, so—so fascinating. All the girls were after him,' she revealed shakily. 'I could hardly believe it when he singled me out for his attention.'

'But *who* was he?'

'Rod Bartlett,' Kathy revealed with trembling reluctance.

'The film star?' she was astounded at the idea.

'He wasn't then, at least only in a small way. He was just starting out, the parts he was being given getting better all the time. He used to live here, Keilly, don't you remember?' She didn't wait for an answer but continued tautly. 'That was how I became friendly with him in London. We were introduced at a party, one of those parties where everyone just turns up whether they're invited or not. Rod found it amusing that we came from the same town and had never really known each other. He may never have realised I existed when he lived in Selchurch,' she remembered bitterly. 'But I certainly knew him. All the girls did; he was popular even then. I thought I was in love with him, and I believed he felt the same way,' she blinked back the tears.

'Yes?' Keilly prompted, never having seen her cousin like this before.

Kathy moved restlessly to her feet, moving to stare sightlessly out of the window. 'Isn't it obvious?' she rasped shrilly. 'He seduced me by telling me he loved me, by making me believe we would get married.' She breathed a ragged sigh. 'I didn't see him again for a few weeks after that, and then I heard—then I heard he had moved in with Veronica King,' she revealed brokenly. 'I wanted to die! Thank God nothing—came of our making love,' she trembled. 'Or I think I *would* have died.'

'You mean a baby?' Keilly gasped, paling.

Kathy's hand shook as she moved it to her hair. 'Yes. He didn't use anything, and I—I suppose he assumed I was on the pill.' She gave a harsh, humourless laugh. 'I'm sure he didn't intentionally run the risk of a paternity suit being brought against him,' she derided bitterly, her gaze suddenly clashing with Keilly's stricken one. 'I'm sorry, love, but now you know why I'm not entitled to wear that white gown Mum insisted I buy, why I'm not a suitable wife for Peter.'

Keilly didn't know what to say, what words of comfort could help her cousin through this crisis in her life. Kathy had only confirmed to her what she had known all her young life, men were takers, thought nothing of deliberately lying to get a woman into bed with them. Rod Bartlett was the one who should have felt guilty, not Kathy!

'Sleeping with one man, because you thought you loved him, doesn't make you promiscuous, Kathy,' she spoke softly. 'I'm sure Peter is understanding enough, mature enough, to realise that.'

Dark brown eyes shadowed over. 'You think I should tell him?'

She shrugged. 'He's going to know tonight anyway,' she sighed.

'But I would be married to him by then!'

'And guilt-stricken, as you are now,' Keilly reminded gently. 'You have to tell him, Kathy, and now, before the wedding this afternoon.'

'So that he has a chance to back out,' Kathy groaned miserably.

'I'm sure he won't do that.' Peter Carmichael was one of the kindest, most understanding men Keilly had ever known, and he loved Kathy enough to forgive her anything.

'Are you?' Kathy said bitterly.

'Darling, you were deceived,' she soothed, feeling the elder one at that moment. 'Rod Bartlett lied to you just to get you into bed with him. You can't be punished for that.'

'Do you really think Peter will see it that way?' she asked uncertainly. 'I couldn't bear it if I lost him now.'

'Talk to him,' she encouraged, completely confident of Peter's reaction.

Kathy had telephoned Peter and arranged to meet him immediately, and when Keilly saw the adoration glowing in Peter's eyes as his bride walked down the aisle towards him she knew she had been right to trust in him, that he had understood.

The young couple had shared a very happy marriage the last six years, had five-year-old Heather as living proof of their love. That Rod Bartlett should now upset the even tenor of Kathy's life again ten years after treating her so callously was despicable.

'He may not even remember you——'

'Is that supposed to console me?' Kathy snapped. 'Oh I suppose you're right,' she sighed. 'Why should a man like that remember one little virgin he seduced ten years ago? But I remember him, Keilly, if he *should* remember me . . .' she trailed off worriedly. 'He could make things very uncomfortable for me.'

'I'm sure Peter would stand by you, after all, he knows there was someone in your past.'

Kathy's gaze was suddenly evasive. 'Keilly, I—I never told him about Rod,' she said in a rush. 'He doesn't know there was ever anyone else.'

'But——'

'I faked it,' Kathy told her heavily.

'F . . . faked it?' she echoed dazedly.

Kathy's beautiful face darkened with irritation. 'It's quite easy to do. And stop looking at me like that, Keilly,' she flushed. 'I *couldn't* tell him. I met him that day, and the first thing he told me was how much he loved me, how proud he was that I was going to be his wife. I couldn't tell him after that, I couldn't lose his respect.'

'But to pretend——! Kathy?' She gave a pained frown.

'I know, I know,' her cousin sighed. 'I've had to live with it for the last six years. Oh I didn't think about it every day,' she dismissed. 'I'm not neurotic about it in that way. But I have had to live with my lie. It hasn't always been easy. Peter is such a wonderful man, and I love him so much, but surely you can understand what it would do to our marriage if he knew I had surrendered myself to a man who probably doesn't remember me among the hundreds of women who have shared his bed?' She shuddered at the thought. 'I won't lose him or Heather because of one silly mistake in my past.'

'Peter would never——'

'No, he wouldn't,' Kathy agreed heavily. 'But a scandal like that about his wife could force us apart. You know his family never really approved of him marrying the daughter of a local hotelier, and a lot of people in this town are just waiting for something like this to happen to our marriage.'

This was the real problem, of course. Peter's family owned most of the town and surrounding land, and when Peter and Kathy had fallen in love nine years ago his family had far from approved of the match. Most of them now accepted the marriage, although as Kathy said, they were just waiting for her to make such a mistake. The fact that Kathy had once had an affair, no matter how briefly, with a 'film star' would certainly cause enough of a scandal to put severe strain on their marriage. Damn Rod Bartlett!

She shook her head. 'I can't say I approve of the fact that you lied to Peter,' she said softly. 'Although in a way I can understand it. But what are we going to do now?' It was her turn for uncertainty. 'What if Rod Bartlett does come back here?'

'Maybe he won't.'

'But if he does?'

'Couldn't you ask this last reporter?' Kathy frowned.

'Rick?' her mouth suddenly felt as dry as her throat, her voice coming out as a nasal rasp.

'Mm,' Kathy seemed unaware of Keilly's unnatural pallor. 'Maybe he's heard something else since he's been back in London. Why don't you telephone him?'

Misery from the flu and the absence of Rick's telephone call settled heavily on her shoulders. 'I don't have his number,' she mumbled.

'Oh,' Kathy still seemed oblivious to Keilly's feelings in her own disappointment. 'Then I suppose we'll just have to sit here and wait,' she sighed.

'Yes,' she gave in to the urge to sneeze, burying her face in a fistful of tissues.

'You poor love,' her cousin sympathised, handing her the nasal spray. 'I shouldn't be bothering you with my problems when you're like this. I'm sure it will all work itself out,' she dismissed confidently.

But no matter how easily Kathy seemed to dismiss the subject of Rod Bartlett Keilly knew her cousin was more deeply affected than she cared to admit. And no wonder, with the admissions she had made! Kathy had been very silly to deceive Peter the way she had, especially after deciding and intending to tell him the truth. For the last six years Keilly had thought the other woman had done exactly that, and it came as a shock to her after all this time to know that she hadn't.

'Why should he want to come here anyway?' Kathy added crossly. 'Selchurch is hardly teeming with the sort of excitement he's used to,' she derided.

She huddled down in the bed, beginning to feel ill again. 'I think that's his main reason; he's taking a holiday, a quiet holiday, for the first time in five years. Let's just hope he finds it boring and doesn't stay long. Maybe you won't even get to meet him! And the chances of him meeting Peter are highly unlikely, Peter's always very busy on the estate.'

'Yes,' her cousin's mouth quirked with taut humour. 'I've had two lovers in my life, one a sex-symbol, the other a hard-working landowner,' her voice broke emotionally. 'God, what a mess,' she groaned. 'I just never imagined there was any possibility of Rod returning to Selchurch.'

'Maybe my letter to the magazine had something to do with it,' she grimaced.

'Don't be silly, love,' Kathy laughed. 'He wouldn't be affected by one damning letter.'

'I don't think he gets many of them,' she said dryly.

'Probably not,' Kathy pulled a face. 'He's a handsome devil with the charm of an angel. I know,' she sighed, 'that sounds contradictory, but not once you've met him, then you will understand.'

'I have no interest in meeting a man like him,' she replied indignantly. 'His sort nauseate me.'

'Oh, Keilly,' her cousin gave a shake of her head. 'I know you had a bad experience in your life, but if you ever met Rod . . .'

'I told you I don't want to meet him!' her voice rose sharply. 'And I hope you aren't getting any silly ideas in your head either,' she added tautly as she saw the faintly reminiscent look in Kathy's eyes.

Kathy's blush was almost one of guilt. 'Of course not,' she snapped, her unusually brittle behaviour not at all reassuring. 'Oh for goodness' sake, Keilly,' she bit out as Keilly continued to look at her with suspicion. 'You think I would risk my marriage for a man like that?'

'No,' she breathed her relief, Kathy's almost dreamy expression of a few minutes ago having her worried for a while. But she wasn't deceived by the other woman's light dismissal of Rod Bartlett either; her cousin still had fond memories of the man, no matter how callously he may have treated her.

Just as she had fond memories of Rick Richards, and he had treated her just as casually. The fact that he hadn't actually made love to her down on the beach was beside the point, they both knew she wouldn't have refused him if he had pressed for her surrender, and although Rick couldn't know it, for her to have done that would have broken a lifetime determination never to be any man's playting. The fact that Rick had been gone now for three days without any word from him more than convinced her that she had been a fool about him.

As the days, and then weeks passed, with it came the conviction that she would never see him again, and then the suspicion that perhaps Barbie hadn't just been the woman who occasionally found him work. Rick had tensed the moment he knew of the other woman's telephone call, as if he hadn't expected her to know where he was. And he had left as soon as he had spoken to the other woman, so perhaps Barbie was his wife?

The more Keilly thought about it the more she realised how he had changed when he knew about the call from the other woman, becoming almost—almost guilty in his actions. Surely only married men reacted that way when contacted by another woman like that, men with something to hide? She decided that the other woman had to be his wife, that she had only been a light diversion for him while he was away from London and his wife's watchful eye.

It was hard to accept that, but after nine weeks went by without a single word from him, not even a Christmas card, she had to believe it. And it hurt. One day she had known him, one evening really, and yet he had made an impression on her previously untouched heart.

She mentally reprimanded herself for being so vulnerable, well aware, with her own fatherless background, ofthe fickleness of men. So she forced herself to settle down to the routine of her life before Rick came, her days spent behind the desk at the hotel, early evenings down at the beach, late evening spent reading a book or watching television. The thought of dating any of the local men didn't interest her at the moment, none of them firing her imagination as Rick had.

The sea became her friend during those nine weeks, reminding her of Rick and the short time they had spent together, the challenge she made of the surging sea now, banishing Rick from her heart each time she battled the water that refused to be beaten. Maybe to Rick their meeting had all been a practised—and well-used—line, but he had been right to liken her to the untamed sea, and during those long lonely weeks since his departure her moods had become as erratic, calm and tranquil one moment, raging furiously the next. She knew she was impossible to live with, that the family treated her warily, and yet she couldn't shake off her black moods of depression, knew that her anger was directed mainly at herself for falling for the seduction of such a man. She may have thought she had found someone special, but all she had found was a lonely husband away from home and looking for a little fun.

'If you promise I won't freeze to death I'll join you.'

She looked up sharply from her sitting position on the sand, in the process of taking off her towelling robe ready for her evening swim. Rick stood several feet away, very like he had on the first and only other night they had ever met, although this time he wasn't wearing the thick sheepskin jacket but a beach-robe similar to her own, his bare legs strong and tanned, covered with a fine sprinkling of dark hair. His beard was still neatly trimmed, although his hair had grown longer, giving him a more rakish air than ever. Lastly she looked at his face, blue eyes twinkling warmly, affecting her in spite of the logical warnings of her brain.

Although it seemed to her as if she had been staring at him for hours she knew her appraisal could only have taken a matter of seconds at the most, schooling her features to remain coolly uninterested. 'I couldn't promise you that,' she returned distantly. 'I haven't been in myself yet.'

'I could hardly believe it when your aunt told me you swim on evenings like this too!'

'If it's warm enough, yes,' she said flatly.

Rick turned narrowed eyes out to the blue-grey sea. 'It looks stormy tonight,' he murmured, almost as if they had only spoken the previous evening and not weeks ago, feeling no awkwardness with her.

'Yes,' she agreed abruptly, although she knew from experience that didn't necessarily mean the water would be icy cold.

The searching gaze returned to her composed features. 'Like you,' he added softly.

Her brows rose. 'I'm perfectly calm,' she replied coolly. 'It's so nice of you to pay us another visit, Mr Richards,' she added politely. 'When did you arrive?'

'About ten minutes ago, I wanted to surprise you.'

Oh he had done that all right! She had begun to accept his absence from her life, not particularly willingly, but she had accepted it had all been a game to him. He had no right to come back here after all this time and act as if he had never been away!

'Did you bring your wife with you this time?' she enquired with sarcastic sweetness.

He looked startled, frowning his puzzlement. 'Wife——? You think a wife is what kept me away from you all these weeks?' He laughed triumphantly, moving forward to swing her up into his arms. 'I don't have a wife, Keilly. Only a woman who reminds me of the sea I love.' He lifted her up against his body until her lips were on a level with his own, holding her effortlessly as he claimed her mouth with a sweet tenderness.

A familiar, and longed for, flood of emotions surged through her body, her arms going about his neck as her fingers became enmeshed in the dark thickness of his hair, its clean silky softness sensuous to the touch. Everything about this man was sensuous, the lean strength of his chest and arms, the stirring arousal of his thighs, the roughess of his bared legs as hers became entwined with his, but most of all the moistly firm lips devouring hers as if he never wanted to stop.

'I missed you, Keilly,' his gaze held hers as he breathed raggedly. 'You frightened the hell out of me just now when you were so cold.' He shook his head. 'I've thought about you all the time I've been away; it's been hell.'

'Then you should have come back sooner.' Sanity was returning slowly, and she struggled to be put down, feeling like a doll that had been picked up to be played with. Reluctantly Rick released her, although he didn't move away, their legs still touching. Keilly stepped back awkwardly. 'Shouldn't you?' her voice was brittle.

His gaze was gentle on her flushed face. 'I was working, Keilly.'

'Oh?' She moved away from him completely, picking up her towel, more for something to do than any real need of it. 'Where did you go?' she mocked. 'A steamy jungle somewhere? The North Pole? Deepest Africa?' her voice had deepened with sarcasm. 'It was somewhere where they didn't have telephones, right?' She scorned his omission to call her as he had said he would.

'No,' he answered quietly.

'I know that,' she said bitterly, her face averted. 'So what are you doing back in Selchurch, Mr Richards? Are you on the trail of yet another story?' she derided.

'You know why I came back, Keilly.'

She feigned surprise. 'I haven't the faintest idea,' she dismissed coolly.

A look of pain flickered in his eyes. 'I've hurt you,' he murmured regretfully.

'Hurt me?' Her eyes flashed, the colour of a storm-tossed sea. 'Don't be ridiculous, Mr Richards. I barely know you,' her mouth twisted with scorn.

Still he didn't move. 'I didn't telephone you because I thought it would just make things worse, for both of us.'

'I don't know what——'

'Keilly!' He swung her round to face him as she would have turned away without interest. 'Don't pretend, darling,' his eyes pleaded with her.

'I really don't know——' her second denial got no further than the last, although this time it was Rick's mouth on hers that stopped her, moving slowly, searchingly, over hers, mastering her with the light thrust of his tongue, deepening the caress as she gave a groan of capitulation, straining up to meet the kiss now.

'I really missed you, Keilly,' he held her face framed in his hands. 'I didn't want to talk to you on the telephone, be able to hear your voice and not be able to touch you. Can you understand that, darling?'

It was all happening too fast again, spiralling out of the control of either of them. 'Yes,' she breathed huskily. 'I understand.'

Rick gave a relieved smile, holding her gently against him. 'I knew you would.'

'How long will you be here this time?' she asked huskily.

'Indefinitely,' he stepped back to look down at her. 'I intend getting to know my sea witch better. Is that all right with you?'

She smiled up at him happily. 'Of course. But can you take the time off from work?'

'Freelance, remember,' he dismissed, looking up as several sea-gulls swooped down overhead.

Keilly admired the gentle strength of his face, the strong column of his throat. She was falling in love with this man, she knew it just as surely as she knew the sun was setting. 'It must be nice to take time off when you feel like it,' she taunted to hide the shock of her discovery.

He turned back to grin at her. 'Hard on the pocket, though,' he smiled. 'Well, are we going for this swim or not?' He arched dark brows at the fast-disappearing sun.

'We are,' she gave a smile of anticipation, imagining his shock when he stepped into the icy cold water. 'I hope you're insured for hypothermia,' she gave a mischievous laugh, throwing off her robe to run down the beach to the water's edge. 'Otherwise you could be in for a nasty surprise.' She ran into the water without waiting for his reaction, striking out forcefully into the waves.

Rick joined her seconds later, seeming none the worse for the coldness of the water, matching his smooth strokes with hers. Keilly had never before had a companion to her evening swim; she enjoyed the challenge of trying to keep up with the power of his body, playing like two seals, Rick's hair curling darkly now that it was wet.

'Enough,' he suddenly decided. 'Or my insurance premium could go up.'

She gave a happy laugh, following him out of the water, swallowing hard as she saw how beautiful he looked in the body-hugging trunks, the black material moulded low down on his hips, his lean body covered with a fine body hair that grew thicker across his chest and lower over his navel. He was beautiful, like a sculpture of a Greek god. Keilly blushed as he turned to see what was delaying her, rushing into speech. 'I bet you didn't get that tan in England.' She picked up her towel, drying herself quickly before pulling on her robe.

He shook his head. 'California. That's where I've been the last nine weeks.'

'Lucky you,' she pulled a face. 'Did you get your story?'

'Yes,' he answered abruptly, dressed himself now. 'We had better get back, it's getting cold now I'm out of the water. Dinner?' he asked as they walked, his arm about her shoulders.

'I can't,' she grimaced her disappointment, remembering she had promised to help Kathy with the organisation of the bazaar in the church hall tonight. It wasn't something she could really get out of, having agreed to help weeks ago. 'Not tonight,' she frowned, thinking quickly. 'But I'm sure Aunt Sylvie won't mind if I have my day off tomorrow instead of Friday,' she suggested with eagerness. 'We only have a couple of guests left over from Christmas. That is—if you would like to spend the day with me?' she added uncertainly, wondering if she had taken too much for granted.

'It's what I'm here for,' he held her close to his side. 'Who's the lucky man tonight?' his tone was casual, too casual.

Keilly felt a warm thrill at his unspoken jealousy. 'A friend I promised to help out,' she teased him.

'Yes?'

Her eyes danced with mischief. 'A female friend.'

'Witch!' Rick bent and kissed her hard on the mouth. 'You'll pay for that tomorrow,' he warned. 'But to tell you the truth, an early night wouldn't be a bad idea,' he held back a tired yawn with effort. 'I only got back from California this morning, and it took me most of the day to drive up here.'

'You must be very tired! You shouldn't——'

'And your concern is encouraging.' He raised

questioning dark brows.

Keilly avoided his glance, too conscious of what had happened between them the last time he was here to offer him too much encouragement. They had time now to get to know each other, could explore more than their physical attraction for each other. 'I really do have to be going now, Rick, otherwise I'm going to be late.'

He nodded. 'Nine o'clock tomorrow?'

'Not too early for you?' she teased.

He returned her smile as they entered the hotel. 'Not too early. Now you had better go and get out of those wet things, your aunt tells me you caught flu just after I left the last time,' he revealed dryly.

Keilly gave him an irritated look. 'That wasn't caused from swimming.'

'No,' he acknowledged throatily. 'Neither was mine,' he added wryly.

'Rick?' She gave a burst of laughter at his confirming nod.

'I love to see you laugh,' he hugged her to him so tightly Keilly felt as if she might break in half. 'Sorry,' he said ruefully at her pained expression. 'But we'll have to choose somewhere a little warmer for our lovemaking next time.' He chuckled as she blushed. 'You're adorable!'

'And you aren't a gentleman,' she pretended anger, feeling self-conscious as two of the other hotel guests walked through the reception area on their way to the dining room. 'I have to go, Rick,' she lightly touched his chest. 'I'll see you in the morning.'

His eyes deepened to navy blue. 'That sounds good,' he murmured softly. 'So good.'

She left him with an embarrassed blush, not knowing how to slow things down between them when Rick said things like that, not even knowing if she wanted to!

He was in the dining room when she hurriedly left twenty minutes later, and she gave him a friendly wave before going out to her car, not having time to do more than that; Kathy was going to be cross with her already for being late, she should have been at the hall half an hour ago.

Kathy gave her a disapproving frown when she rushed into the cold hall a few minutes later, both women dressed in denims and sweaters for the task ahead of them.

'Before you say anything, I'm sorry,' Keilly sighed, throwing off her gloves and coat.

'I wouldn't mind,' her cousin said tightly. 'But every time it's the same, people promise to come and help and they never do. The committee I can understand, but I didn't ask you, Keilly, you offered.'

'Yes, I know. But——'

'Just look at this mess,' Kathy groaned at the bags of goods that surrounded them. 'It's been arriving all day, and I don't even know where to start.'

'Don't worry,' she soothed. 'It's always like this, you know that. It won't take long to organise once we get started.' She was already sorting goods out on one of the trestle tables that had been put up for the occasion. 'No one else has arrived at all?'

'No,' Kathy sighed. 'They make me the chairwoman of these committees and then leave me to do the work. It's always the same,' she mumbled. 'I don't know why I agree to do it.'

'Because you love it,' she chided, receiving a wry smile in reply.

Her certainty of it not taking long proved correct, and pretty soon they had things sorted to the appropriate tables, Kathy's tension easing as they neared the end of their task, the two of them sitting down to a well-earned rest and a cup of tea when they finished shortly after eleven o'clock.

'Mm, thanks,' Kathy accepted her cup gratefully. 'Thank goodness that's over, I'm sure it gets worse every time. You never did tell me why you were late,' she eyed Keilly curiously.

She had thought herself beyond coy blushes, but just thinking of Rick was enough to make the colour flood her cheeks. 'Rick came back,' she didn't attempt to prevaricate, knowing her expression must give her away.

'He did?' Kathy said sharply, lowering her cup down on to her knee.

She smiled her pleasure. 'Yes.'

'And?'

Keilly looked puzzled. 'And?' she echoed.

Her cousin sighed her impatience. 'It's been a long day, Keilly, in fact it's been a long couple of months,' her brittle tone was evidence of her renewed tension, 'and I'll take a bet on your not even asking this Rick if he's heard any more about Rod's plans.'

She gasped her dismay, blushing her guilt.

'I knew it,' Kathy sighed again, standing up wearily. 'I've been worrying myself sick the last two months and you didn't even give Rod Bartlett another thought, did you?' she snapped accusingly.

It wasn't true that she hadn't thought of the actor over the last weeks, she had, but as soon as she saw Rick again she completely forgot the film star's existence. 'I'm sorry, Kathy,' she grimaced. 'Although I can ask him in the morning. He says he's staying on for a while,' she revealed softly.

Kathy was so deeply immersed in her own worrying thoughts that she didn't notice Keilly's happiness at the thought of a prolonged visit by Rick. 'Well I wish you would ask him,' she said with biting sarcasm. 'I'd be interested,' she understated.

'I really am sorry,' she groaned her dismay. 'I just never thought . . . Rick didn't mention anything about Rod Bartlett,' she added as if to vindicate herself, very much aware that she had gone down several notches in her cousin's estimation. 'I'll call you as soon as I've spoken to him.'

'Thanks,' Kathy sounded preoccupied now, taking their cups through to the kitchen to wash them through. 'I think we've finished here for now, would you mind dropping me off at home? Peter has the car this evening.'

'Kathy——'

'Shall we go?' she asked briskly. 'I'm sure you must be as tired as I am.'

She wished there were something she could do, something she could say to make up for her lapse, but only talking to Rick could do that, and that would have to wait until the morning. It had been thoughtless of her not to think of Kathy's worry, her cousin had obviously been under severe strain the last two months, had even been short-tempered with Heather a couple of times, something that usually never happened. She just hadn't given Rod Bartlett's involvement with Kathy any thought once she saw Rick again and they had established how much they had missed each other. She would have to correct that oversight and call Kathy before she and Rick went out tomorrow.

She sorted through the mail as she waited for him to come downstairs the next morning, her aunt agreeing to take over as soon as she wanted to leave.

'Good morning, my darling,' Rick nuzzled his face into her throat as his arms came about her from behind, his body hard against her as he bent into her.

'Rick!' she squirmed, half in pleasure, half in embarrassment at someone coming in and finding them in such a compromising position. 'Not here,' she protested as he made no effort to release her. 'Someone could see us—There's something different about you!' She put her hand up to caress his cheek. 'Your beard!' she gasped. 'It's gone!'

'It may not have tickled,' he growled against her ear. 'But it certainly itched. I'm glad to get rid of it at last, it's been six months of discomfort.'

'Then why grow it?' she still touched the smoothness of his jaw, leaning back against him.

'Because I don't like false beards.'

'False——?' She pulled out of his arms to turn and look at him with a puzzled frown, her eyes widening as she looked not at Rick but at a complete stranger, a stranger she knew and yet didn't know.

'I'd be glad to give you a private viewing of "any part of my anatomy" any time you feel in the mood,' Rod Bartlett winked at her suggestively.

CHAPTER THREE

KEILLY stared at him in numbed shock. The voice was surely Rick's, but the face, the face was known to millions as Rod Bartlett, film star and sex symbol. Without the beard the lean length of his jaw was visible, the firm sensuousness of his mouth. There could be no doubting it, Rick, the Rick she had found so devastatingly attractive, was in truth Rod Bartlett.

Her eyes chilled to an icy grey, her mouth firming to hostility. 'Very funny, Mr Bartlett,' she said with smooth sarcasm. 'What do you do for an encore?' she asked coldly.

'Keilly——'

'And to think we've had Rod Bartlett staying with us not once but twice,' she moved behind the protection of the reception desk, her legs shaking so badly she was glad of its support as she leant weakly against it. 'You honour us, Mr Bartlett.'

'Keilly——'

'Maybe we could put up a plaque or something, "Rod Bartlett stayed here". Or better yet, "Rod Bartlett slept here",' she taunted with bitterness. 'Think of the guests we could attract, women of course, who would like to sleep in the same bed Rod Bartlett did. Yes,' her voice rose shrilly. 'It certainly is an idea. I'll have to suggest it to my——'

'Keilly, that is enough!' Rick—or Rod, spoke sternly, glancing round impatiently as an elderly couple approached the desk, moving aside to study the notice-board as they lingered to pay their bill.

Keilly spoke to the couple with her usual politeness, even actively engaged them in conversation to keep them from leaving, and all the time she did her thoughts were racing. If Rick was really Rod Bartlett—and there could be no doubt that he was!—then what had he been doing here in Selchurch the first time? What was he doing here this time, for that matter? Rick Richards she had been inclined to give the benefit of the doubt, to believe that he had come back because he was attracted to her, but Rod Bartlett——! She wasn't inclined to give him the benefit of the doubt about anything!

And least of all his being attracted to *her*. Since Veronica King had killed herself six years ago there had been a stream of women in Rod Bartlett's life, all of them beautiful, usually as much in the limelight as he was himself, attracting twice the publicity to their romance.

'Let's get out of here now,' he came back to the desk to growl as soon as the elderly couple were out of earshot.

Keilly looked up from the invoice she had been filing. 'Go, Mr Bartlett?' she met his gaze with accusing eyes. 'Didn't the letter I wrote to the magazine, and our conversation the last time you were here, tell you exactly what I think of Rod Bartlett?' she scorned. 'I have no intention of going anywhere with such a man.'

'And Rick Richards?' he grated.

Her mouth tightened. 'I think we can all agree that he was a figment of our imaginations——'

'Ah, Mr Richards,' her aunt appeared from the kitchen. 'I hope I haven't delayed the two of you too much,' she took over from Keilly behind the desk. 'Well off you go,' she encouraged as Keilly made no move to leave. 'It's a lovely day for January, so I should go now and make the most of it. It will probably rain later,' she laughed ruefully. 'Are you going anywhere special?' she asked with interest.

'I——'

'We thought we would just drive for a while and see where it takes us,' Rod Bartlett was the one to answer her, taking a firm hold of Keilly's arm and almost dragging her towards the door.

'Have a good time,' her aunt called lightly.

Keilly pulled out of his grasp as soon as they were outside, glaring her dislike of him. 'Don't touch me,' she spat the words at him. 'I'm not going anywhere with you.'

'We have to talk——'

'What about?' she snapped. 'You've had your little game, Mr Bartlett,' she scorned, looking very beautiful in that moment, her eyes a dark sparkling grey, a healthy glow to her cheeks in her anger. 'Your acting was excellent, as usual,' she added with dry sarcasm. 'I'm only sorry you won't get nominated for an Oscar for it.'

'I'm already nominated for one,' he rasped.

'For "Beginning Again"?'

'As a matter of fact, yes,' he bit out. 'I'm going over for the presentation in April.'

'So sure you're going to win?'

Anger flared briefly in the deep blue eyes. 'Polite enough to go there personally if I'm nominated.'

She flushed at the rebuke, and then chastised herself for feeling in the least guilty for thinking badly of this man. She knew too much about him, his fatal betrayal of Veronica King, his selfish seduction of Kathy. He deserved every bit of scorn she felt!

'I'm sure your adoring public will be ecstatic,' she derided. 'You're sure to win.'

'Keilly, I'm not going to stand here discussing some damned Oscar when I——'

'Really, Mr Bartlett, what would your peers think of your attitude to their accolade to you?'

He heaved a deep sigh at her unhidden sarcasm. 'When I really want to talk to you about something completely different,' he finished determinedly. 'And we *are* going to talk.' Once again he grasped her arm, pushing her in the direction of the car park.

Her eyes widened with derisive appreciation as he took her over to a silver-grey Jaguar sports car. 'You didn't bring this with you last time,' she mocked. 'I would have remembered it.'

He flashed her a look of irritation before thrusting her into the passenger side, climbing in next to her to start the engine with a roar, speeding out on to the road and away from the hotel. 'Last time I was here I flew up as far as Liverpool and then hired a car,' he revealed tightly, driving with concentration, seeming to know where he was going.

'How inconvenient for you!' Keilly stared fixedly ahead, and yet she still knew every detail about the man at her side, knew that the clothes she had guessed to be expensive the first time he was here were really designer jeans and a silk shirt, that the longer casually windswept styling of his hair had been achieved by an expert, and that the chunky gold medallion he wore at his throat probably cost a fortune. She knew all that about him now, now that she knew he was Rod Bartlett.

'It was a little,' he replied tautly. 'I was taking a break from my latest film when Barbie suggested I come up here and see for myself the lady who had taken such an intense dislike to me.'

'I'm flattered,' her tone implied she was anything but that. 'Although I'm surprised you bothered.' Once again she wondered what Barbie was to him, although she made no mention of the other woman. She was *not* jealous, damn it! She despised this man, and his lifestyle, and that wasn't only because of what he had done to Kathy in the past.

His expression was grim, the lean hand moving the wheel with the minimum of effort. 'The publicity abroad and here reached embarrassing proportions.'

'How awful for you!'

'Keilly,' he sighed. 'I'm just trying to explain the situation to you. The press were speculating all sorts of things, and I must admit I began to wonder myself. Your name sounded familiar——'

'We had never met before,' she told him sharply, paling slightly.

'No, I realised that the moment I saw you. I still don't know why you disliked me so much you had to put it in writing,' he frowned, the beautiful blue eyes puzzled.

'*Dislike*,' she amended. 'The feeling is still very much in the present tense. Your deceit in coming here under an assumed name just confirms my opinion of you. But at least now you'll be able to tell the "speculating" press that I'm merely a vindictive woman hitting out at you. After all, if anyone ever asks I won't be able to deny that we've met, that we've made love.'

'That isn't why I kissed you, damn it,' he grated. 'Being attracted to you was the last thing on my mind when I came here. And it isn't an assumed name, I sometimes choose to use only part of it, but my full name is Rod*erick* Richard Bartlett.'

'What a mouthful!'

'Exactly,' he bit out tautly. 'Admittedly I usually use the name Rod Richards when I don't want to be recognised, but I thought you were too intelligent for that.'

'How nice!'

'Keilly, for God's sake! You liked me when I was Rick Richards,' he rasped. 'What's so different about me now?'

Now she knew him as a seducer, a man who was totally selfish, a man not unlike her father had been! 'If you don't know then I'm not going to tell you,' she snapped.

'What sort of stupid answer is that?'

Her eyes flashed deeply grey. 'The only one I can think of at the moment! How did you expect me to react to the truth about you?' she demanded accusingly. 'Forget everything that I—I wrote about you?' her words were vehement as she realised the slip she had almost made, almost revealing what she knew about his treatment of Kathy. 'Be flattered and excited that a famous film star deigned to kiss me one night on a deserted beach? Is that what you thought?'

His hands tightly gripped the steering wheel. 'If it were, I would hardly have bothered to come back,' he said between clenched teeth.

The tautness of his jaw made Keilly a witness of the famous cleft in the hard chin, Rod Bartlett's sex appeal was something that couldn't be denied. 'You told me yourself,' she shrugged. 'You need a holiday, a quiet holiday.'

'It never occurred to me to come back to Selchurch until I met you.'

'I won't be your summer affair, Mr Bartlett—Oh!' she groaned her surprised pain as he swerved the powerful car off the road, knocking her arm against the door as they bumped over the uneven ground to the hilltop that overlooked the little town.

He stared straight ahead for several minutes after switching off the engine, his hands still on the steering-wheel, his shoulders tensed. 'You're angry,' he began to relax a little, talking in a controlled voice. 'And I can understand why. But I don't want you for a summer affair,' he turned in his seat to look at her, the console separating them. 'There are plenty of women back in London who would be only too ready to oblige if that were all I wanted,' he said without conceit. 'I want more than that from you, Keilly——'

'I'm not even willing to offer *that* much,' she pushed open the door to get out of the car, moving to the side of the hill, looking down on the town that had been her home all her life. She loved this little town, she belonged here, and she could understand in that moment how Kathy had been so impressed with the glamour and excitement a young actor in London must have shown to her small-town inexperience. She could understand it, but she wasn't about to repeat it!

She sensed Rod Bartlett's presence beside her, kept her face expressionless as she gazed down at the calm blue-grey sea that for once didn't reflect her mood, her thoughts stormy, her hands clenching and unclenching in her denims' pockets.

'Keilly——' he swore under his breath as she flinched away from him before moving several feet away with pointed distaste. 'Just because my name had changed doesn't mean I have too,' a nerve pulsed erratically in the shaven smoothness of his jaw, 'I wanted you nine weeks ago, and I want you now.'

Her mouth twisted, tears glistening in her eyes for the way she had been deceived. 'The same way you've wanted all those other women you've "relaxed" with the last ten or twelve years?' she reminded him of the way he had described Rod Bartlett's numerous affairs the last time he had been here. 'Thanks, but no thanks, Mr Bartlett.'

'Afraid you might get hurt?' he flared.

She shook her head with cool disdain. 'Not interested in taking a number.'

'Why you——'

'Careful, Mr Bartlett,' she taunted. 'Your ego is showing.'

He gave a ragged sigh. 'I'm sorry,' he said abruptly. 'Losing my temper with you is not going to help the situation.'

'As I see it there is no situation,' she dismissed. 'You're a guest in my aunt and uncle's hotel, and as such I'm required to be polite to you in my professional capacity. Personally, that's a different matter,' she added stiltedly. 'Then I would prefer it if you left me completely alone.'

'I can't do that,' he told her grimly.

'Why not?' she frowned.

'You know why,' he said heavily. 'Contrary to what you think, what you want to believe, all my responses to you have been genuine. Admit it, Keilly, if I were still Rick Richards you wouldn't be doubting my feelings in this way.'

She blushed at the truth of that. 'But you aren't, are you,' she reminded stiffly. 'You're Rod Bartlett, the man hundreds of women claim to have slept with, one of them even committed suicide for you.'

He seemed to pale at the last accusation, a pulse beating in his jaw. 'Hundreds is an exaggeration,' he bit out tautly. 'As for Veronica——'

'You talk about her as if she didn't matter!' Keilly accused heatedly.

His eyes flashed deeply blue, his lashes long and sooty. 'I loved her,' the statement was made so simply it couldn't possibly be doubted. 'She was the best thing that ever happened to me. At the time I met her I was drifting, using people as they used me, my career going nowhere. Veronica put me back together, showed me that being true to myself, to my beliefs, was all that really mattered when it came down to it. I loved her,' he repeated huskily.

Keilly swallowed hard at his quiet sincerity, forcing herself to remember the way the other woman had died. 'It's amazing how your career suddenly took off once you were her live-in-lover,' she said with sarcasm, ignoring the dangerous darkening of his expression. 'Yes, I'm sure you "loved" her very much,' she derided.

He thrust his hands into his hair, as if he might strike her if he didn't. 'I wanted to marry her, but she refused,' he revealed tightly.

Her eyes widened slightly at this admission, although she hardened her heart once again. This man was still the user he had been then, would always be. 'Maybe she just didn't want to be used any more,' Keilly scorned.

His mouth thinned, his eyes becoming glacial. 'Make your mind up, Keilly,' he rasped. 'I'm either the user who discarded Veronica when she was no longer useful, or I'm the man she spurned as a husband,' his mouth twisted. 'I can't be both.'

'You—You—You're a totally selfish man!' she accused hotly. 'And I don't believe for one moment you asked Veronica King to marry you. Why would she commit suicide if that were the case?'

'Why indeed?' he echoed softly.

Keilly gave him a searching look. 'She *did* commit suicide.'

'Yes,' he didn't dispute the claim.

'Because of you!'

He gave a controlled sigh. 'In part,' he nodded. 'Although not for the reasons you think,' he added sharply. 'Maybe one day, if the two of us ever sort out our differences, I'll tell you all about Veronica.'

'That day will never come,' she said with vehemence, knowing from his callous treatment of Kathy how selfish he was. Maybe he truly believed he had changed from the drifter and user he had been then, but he had still crushed people underfoot to achieve it.

'I have to disagree with you,' he shrugged. 'I have to believe that one day we'll be together. And when that time comes we'll talk about Veronica. I'm sure she wouldn't mind in the circumstances.'

'Why not now?' she frowned.

'It's all a question of trust, Keilly,' he held her gaze with steady blue eyes. 'And when you learn to trust me—again, I'll know the time is right to tell you the truth about Veronica and myself.'

'And all those other women you've slept with?' she taunted with distaste.

'I told you, there haven't been so many, and most—although I'm not claiming all,' he added grimly. 'Knew there was no future in the relationship.'

'And the ones that didn't?'

'I'm not claiming to be a saint, Keilly,' he snapped, a dark hue to his lean cheeks. 'I've hurt people, I'm aware of that, but then so has everyone. We're all fallible, we all make mistakes.'

'Only you don't pay for yours, the woman does!'

He searched her flushed face with a probing glance. 'I haven't left a trail of fatherless children behind me, if that's what you believe,' he bit out, his mouth twisting with derision. 'Believe me, I would have heard about it by now if I had.'

She knew what he meant; there had been a lot of paternity cases brought against people who were prominent in the media, and his name had so far been noticeably absent considering the amount of affairs he was reputed to have had. But she also knew of his carelessness with Kathy! 'Maybe you've just been lucky,' she dismissed abruptly, knowing the penalty paid by people like him.

'And maybe I haven't,' he rasped. 'Keilly, that was all in the past, it's the future we should concern ourselves with.'

'What future?'

'The one we're going to have,' he moved so close their legs almost touched. 'I told you, Keilly, we're going to be together.'

'You——' Her denial was effectively cut off by Rod Bartlett's mouth coming down on hers.

It was useless fighting him, he was much stronger than she was, but she didn't offer him any response or encouragement either. She wanted to, God how she wanted to, but pride and common sense made her hold out. This man may be jaded with his London life, be a little bored with his sophisticated friends, but she wasn't about to provide him with a little light amusement.

Then the pressure of his mouth on hers began to change, no longer taking from her but asking for a response with the light caress of his lips as he nibbled on hers, taking the lower lip fully into his mouth with an eroticism that made her shudder in reaction, her body melting into his as she groaned her capitulation.

'Keilly, Keilly,' he muttered her name over and over again as his mouth travelled the length of her throat, his strong hands caressing the curve of her spine as he held her into him.

She felt his hands against her bare skin beneath her cotton shirt, gasping as one of those hands cupped beneath her bare breast, his thumbtip moving lightly across the peak, the nipple surging to pulsating life beneath the sensitive caress. Warmth spread through her body at the intimacy of his caress, no other man ever touching her in this way.

'God, Keilly, how I want and need you—Keilly?' his voice sharpened as she pushed away from him, his hands straining her back against him.

'Let me go,' she ordered through gritted teeth.

'Didn't you hear me? I said——'

'I *heard*,' she managed to wrench away from him, breathing hard in her agitation, the tautness of her breasts thrusting against the cotton material of her shirt. 'You must think me very stupid, Mr Bartlett——'

'I don't think you're anything at the moment, because I don't understand you!' he stared at her as if he had never seen her before. 'Do you always react this way when a man tells you how much he needs you?' he frowned.

'No other man ever has,' she bit out. 'And I certainly don't want to hear it from you,' she refused to acknowledge the way he seemed to pale at her words. 'I may be naïve,' she continued hardly. 'But I'm not some impressionable teenager that will be taken in by a line like that——'

'Line . . .?' he repeated icily.

'What else would you call it?' she scorned. 'God, did you think I was so stupid, a dumb idiot from the backwoods that you could fool along until it was time for you to leave here? And then what would you have said about needing me, that it was another one of those mistakes you seem to keep making, that we should part for a while to see how we really feel about each other? I saw that film,' she scoffed. 'The heroine never saw the hero again!'

'This isn't a film,' he told her heatedly. 'This is real

life, yours and mine, and I don't play scenes from films in my life.'

'You could have fooled me—*could* have,' she repeated mockingly. 'But I'm really not that stupid. Now if you don't mind I'd like to go back to town. I have the time off anyway, so I think I'll spend some of it on the beach.'

'Keilly, listen to me——'

'The water is probably still too cold at the moment, but I could take a walk along the beach,' she continued as if he hadn't spoken. 'I wonder——'

'Keilly, will you listen to me!'

She looked at him with cool grey eyes. 'Not if you're going to tell me you need me again,' she told him flatly. 'I doubt you *need* anyone. I hope you enjoy your stay here, Mr Bartlett, I'm sure there must be a lot of your old friends who would just love to see you. I hope you'll understand if I prefer not to be counted in their number, I simply don't have the time for world-weary superstars looking for a new thrill.'

His jaw tightened at her insulting tone, but there was no other visible evidence of his burning anger. 'You may not be a child, Keilly,' he ground out slowly. 'But you certainly think like one, *world-weary superstar*,' he derided. 'Do you have any idea how ridiculous you sound?'

'No more ridiculous than you did a few minutes ago, I can assure you!' she flared.

He flushed, sighing heavily. 'I can see there's no point in talking to you now. I'll see you again once you've calmed down.'

'I'm completely calm,' she told him evenly. 'And if you aren't ready to go back yet I think I'll walk.'

'There's no need for that,' he said tautly, turning to go back to the car, sitting behind the wheel to wait for her to join him.

Her movements weren't as fluid as usual, too conscious of brooding blue eyes watching her progress, climbing in beside him as the engine roared into life, staring wordlessly ahead as they drove back down the coastal road.

She had to blink back the tears so that he shouldn't see how much his betrayal had hurt her. Rod Bartlett! God, it was like a nightmare. And she had believed she was falling in love with him! The fact that he was who he was had ended that, she couldn't feel anything for the man who had so calculatingly seduced Kathy before going to a woman who could give him so much more—until she too became dispensable. He said he didn't act in real life, well he had certainly been doing a good job of pretending since the moment they had met, to be a kind and sensitive man, something he could never be in reality!

'Thank you,' she said stiltedly as he stopped the car outside the hotel.

'Keilly!' His hand on her arm stopped her getting out. 'I mean it,' he told her quietly as she looked at him with wide questioning eyes. 'I need you more than I've ever needed anyone in my life before.'

She flushed. 'Please save that routine for some poor idiot who will believe you,' she sighed wearily. 'It's wasted on me.'

He drove off as soon as she stepped out on to the pavement, and with a ragged sigh she at last allowed the tension to flow out of her. He hadn't even used an original approach with her, had used the same line with her as he had with Kathy all those years ago.

Kathy. Dear God, she had to see Kathy straight away, had to warn her cousin that Rod Bartlett was indeed back in town!

The Hall was a warm and happy place in spite of its

size, Kathy making the huge country estate into a home for her husband and daughter. Although her welcoming smile as she opened the door herself turned to a look of anxiety as she saw Keilly.

'I've been waiting for you to call me all morning,' she dragged Keilly through to the comfort of the small sitting room she always used for friends and family.

'It's only ten-thirty,' she delayed, standing nervously in front of the unlit fireplace.

Kathy grimaced. 'When you've been up since six that seems a long time.'

Her brows rose. 'You had an early start today?'

'Heather has been coughing most of the night. I think she's getting a chest cold,' Kathy shrugged. 'I've kept her at home today.'

'She's upstairs?'

'Sleeping,' her cousin nodded. 'Have you seen Rick again?' her voice was taut.

'Oh yes,' she sighed raggedly. 'I've seen him.'

'And?'

She moistened her lips. 'Rod Bartlett is coming back to Selchurch,' she announced firmly. 'In fact,' she paused hesitantly as Kathy sank into a chair. 'He's already back.'

Kathy's hand shook as she nervously fidgeted with her already immaculate hair. 'I—Rick told you that? Or have you seen him?' Her eyes widened to haunted brown pools.

'Both,' she sighed, going over to sit on the floor at her cousin's feet. 'Kathy, Rick *is* Rod Bartlett. He——'

'What do you mean?' her cousin demanded sharply. 'I don't understand. You said this Rick was a reporter, that he came here after a story.'

'Because that's what he told me,' she nodded bitterly.

'He lied to me, was playing some cruel game of his own.'

'You're sure he is—Of course you're sure,' Kathy sighed raggedly at her own stupidity. 'Rod Bartlett is easily recognisable.'

'Without a beard, yes,' Keilly acknowledged heavily. 'And he doesn't have a beard now. I'm sorry, Kathy, I had no idea who he was.' That was surely the understatement of the year!

'Had you—told him anything about me?'

'Of course not,' she said impatiently. 'Our conversations hardly went as far as reminiscing about the women he knew in the past,' she snapped. 'And I'm not likely to have volunteered any information about you, now am I?'

'No,' Kathy sighed. 'I'm just so edgy at the moment, I don't know what I'm saying. Do you know how long he intends staying?' She looked anxious.

'Indefinitely, he said. But I shouldn't take too much notice of that,' she added hastily as her cousin seemed to pale even more. 'At the time he said it he believed I would be willing to—to share his summer with him.' She blushed at her cousin's probing look. 'Needless to say I'm not,' she mumbled.

'Keilly——'

'Could I go up and see Heather?' she asked brightly. 'She could be awake now.'

'I suppose so,' Kathy said crossly. 'I must say, you don't seem too concerned with the fact that he was making a fool out of you.'

Her eyes flashed deeply grey. 'What good would it do me?' she snapped.

'All the same——'

'Look, let's forget it, Kathy,' she sighed. 'I've made sure Mr Bartlett knows exactly what I think of him; I don't think he'll be bothering me again,' she added dully, sure that she was right. Why should a man like him go to the trouble of pursuing someone who obviously wasn't willing when it was equally as obvious there were hundreds—no, thousands—who were only *too* willing.

'He can be very persistent,' Kathy muttered. 'Why on earth did you get involved with him, Keilly?' she demanded accusingly, looking flustered again. 'If he wants you he'll stay here until he gets you.'

'You make it sound as if I have no say in the matter!'

'*I* didn't,' Kathy mumbled bitterly.

Contrition at once washed over her; she shouldn't be indulging in her own unhappiness but thinking of Kathy's dilemma. If Rod did stay here the chances of him and Kathy meeting were increased tremendously, worse, he could even meet Peter. 'I'm sorry, love,' she touched her cousin's arm consolingly. 'I wasn't thinking. But I'm sure Mr Bartlett won't stay——'

'Mr Bartlett?' Peter queried lightly as he came into the room, seemingly oblivious to the fact that both women looked stricken by his unexpected appearance. 'Hello, darling,' he kissed his wife warmly before kissing Keilly on the cheek. 'Day off?'

'Er—yes,' she nodded awkwardly.

'Quite nice weather for January,' he said with his usual enthusiasm for life, tall and handsome, with short blond hair and laughing blue eyes. It was his warmth and genuine caring for people that made him so popular with his employees and the town people. 'Was that Rod Bartlett you were talking about?'

Keilly paled, swallowing hard. 'Why do you ask?' she delayed, wondering what had made him think of the celebrated actor.

'Well I heard he was in town——'

'You did?' Kathy squeaked.

Peter smiled, mistaking his wife's distress for awed disbelief. 'Mrs Groves mentioned it when I called in at the shop a few minutes ago, she's sure he was in there this morning,' he sounded a little sceptical.

'He probably was,' Keilly said dully, aware that the gossip and speculation as to the reason the actor was in town had already started; it could only get worse!

'Really?' Peter asked interestedly. 'You mean he really is in Selchurch?'

She glanced at Kathy, knowing by her pale face and drawn features that this was all a little too much for her, that she could crack under the strain at any moment. 'He's staying at the hotel,' she revealed reluctantly, all the time keeping a watchful eye on her cousin. 'He arrived yesterday.'

'Oh dear,' Peter's brows rose in sympathy. 'Isn't that a little embarrassing for you?'

She knew he was referring to the letter she had written to the magazine, the incident had been as much of a nine-day-wonder here as it had in the rest of the country. 'A little,' she admitted stiffly. 'Although Mr Bartlett doesn't seem concerned by it, in fact he finds it quite amusing,' she added hardly.

'That's good.' Peter nodded his approval of the other man's behaviour. 'I wonder if he might be persuaded to do something at the Easter Fête,' he murmured thoughtfully. 'He could be a big drawing attraction——'

'Really, Peter,' Kathy's voice was brittle with sarcasm, her eyes overbright as she held on to her control with effort. 'The man is here on holiday.'

Her husband looked slightly puzzled by her vehemence. 'I know that, darling. I just thought——'

'I can't understand what all the fuss is about,' she dismissed tautly. 'He may be famous, but he's only a man, for all that. You've always told me it's a person's deeds that count, Peter,' her voice was becoming shrill.

'Yes. But——'

'Well surely Mr Bartlett's exploits over the years far from indicate any interest in doing charity work?' she taunted hardly. 'I'm taking it for granted that we couldn't pay him anything.'

Keilly could see Peter's dismay with Kathy's unusual behaviour, and rushed to her cousin's aid. 'Why don't you and I go up and see how Heather is, Peter, and Kathy can make us all a nice cup of tea?' The last was added as a way of giving Kathy time alone to collect her shattered thoughts together. Luckily her cousin took it!

'That sounds like a good idea,' Kathy said with feigned brightness. 'Perhaps Mrs Scott has made some of your favourite biscuits too, darling. Five minutes,' she warned lightly as they went up the stairs.

Keilly could sense the puzzlement in the sensitive man at her side, although Peter said nothing as they went upstairs, was teasing and loving to his young daughter as she obviously still felt a little feverish. But Keilly wasn't deceived by Peter's mild manner, he was too much of a man attuned to people's emotions not to know of his wife's tension.

'Keilly,' his hand on her arm stopped their progress down the stairs once they left Heather's room. 'Do you have any idea what's troubling Kathy?' he sounded worried.

She chewed on her inner lip. 'Maybe it's just the winter blues,' she dismissed. 'It always seems to last so long.'

'Maybe that's it.' But he didn't sound convinced. 'Are the two of you going shopping today? That usually helps cheer Kathy up,' he said indulgently.

Both of them knew of Kathy's enthusiasm and weakness for shopping, Keilly laughing too. 'I'll suggest it to her,' she nodded.

'I wish you would,' he squeezed her arm gratefully. 'It might help cheer her up.'

She doubted that, but she made the suggestion anyway, persuading Kathy that going out was better than staying in. And with Heather asleep once again, and the housekeeper in close attendance, it was difficult for her to refuse. But Kathy tried.

'You heard Peter,' she said moodily. 'The damned man is wandering around the town. What if we run into him?'

'What if we do?' she soothed, not exactly welcoming the idea herself, not after the way they had parted earlier.

'He could recognise me!'

'After ten years?' she scoffed. 'Is that likely?'

'You tell me,' Kathy's voice was shrill again. 'Have I changed much in those years?'

If anything her cousin was more beautiful than she had been then, but that was beside the point now. Keilly gave an impatient sigh. 'Whether or not you've changed doesn't matter, *if* he should decide to stay you can't hide at The Hall all the time he's here; Peter would think that decidedly odd!'

It took a little persuading but Kathy finally saw the wisdom of her words, although she spent all of the time they were out looking about them as if she were being hunted.

'Peter's worried about you,' Keilly warned when they returned from the shops. 'He'll be even more worried if you continue to act like this.' Kathy hadn't stopped pacing since they got back.

'How can you possibly understand how I feel?'

Kathy's eyes flashed angrily. 'One indiscretion in my past, and it could ruin the rest of my life!'

She hid the pain her cousin's thoughtless words had inflicted, knowing that Kathy had forgotten the indiscretion in the past that *had* ruined her life!

But she was no more enamoured of seeing Rod Bartlett again than her cousin was, she knew that she had made a fool of herself over him in a way she had sworn would never happen to her. She hoped Rod Bartlett had found his cruelty worth it.

She didn't know what her feelings were when she got back to the hotel to find he had booked out of the hotel that afternoon!

CHAPTER FOUR

THE promise to attend the bazaar had been made at the same time she had offered to help Kathy arrange it all, and although she didn't feel in the least like attending she accompanied her aunt on Saturday afternoon, leaving her uncle in charge of the more or less empty hotel. Now that Rod had left so abruptly their only remaining guests were a young married couple who had eyes and ears only for each other. Keilly thought the couple were on their honeymoon, although they were trying to keep it low-key.

About Rod's departure she tried not to dwell too much. She had known his declaration of needing her had been a well-used line, but nevertheless it was more than a little galling—so *much* more than that!—that he hadn't even tried to stay around another day or so to try and persuade her to change her mind about an affair with him. Not that she would ever have agreed, but he could have *tried*, damn him!

For Kathy's sake she felt glad he had left, for her own—she was torn in two about her feelings for him. As Rick Richards he had been the only man ever to understand her affinity with the elements, as Rod Bartlett he had once hurt Kathy beyond measure, and made a fool out of her too. If only she didn't have so much trouble reconciling herself to the fact that the two men were one person.

Her aunt had no such reservation. 'What a surprise, Mr Richards being Rod Bartlett all the time,' she had remarked over breakfast.

'Yes,' Keilly answered abruptly, a sleepless night leaving her feeling heavy eyed and listless, not in the least like attending what promised to be a noisy bazaar.

Her aunt gave her a sympathetic look. 'It must have been embarrassing for you, darling, and once you had met him you seemed to like him so much,' she gave Keilly a probing look.

'Yes,' she acknowledged again, her buttered toast suddenly having the consistency of soggy cardboard. 'But he's gone now, so we can forget he was ever here.' She could hardly wait to tell Kathy of his departure.

'Hm,' her aunt agreed, although she didn't look convinced as to Keilly's genuine relief.

The bazaar was well under way by the time they arrived, although they could see no sign of Kathy. Not that this was so surprising, Kathy was usually in the thick of it at this sort of occasion, as head of the committee she was expected to be.

'Grandma, Grandma!' Heather suddenly appeared out of the crowd, dancing up and down in her excitement. 'Come and look at the lovely cakes.'

'I take it you're feeling better,' Keilly teased her.

The little girl gave an impish grin, taking hold of each of one of their hands. 'Much,' she nodded. 'Will you come and look at the cakes?' she prompted again.

'I'll join you in a moment,' Keilly promised. 'I just have to find Mummy. Do you know where she is?'

'Making tea,' the little girl supplied.

'I'll see you both later.' She started to make her way over to the kitchen, which took a lot longer than it should have done, friends and acquaintances she hadn't seen for some time stopping her for a chat.

She smiled her excuses to one of the women who helped out at the hotel during the summer months, turning sharply to bump into the man standing directly behind her. 'I'm sorry! I——' the smile of apology froze on her lips as she looked up into teasing blue eyes. 'Rod . . .!' she gasped, knowing she had paled. 'I thought you had left.'

His strong hands came up to steady her, drawing her to one side of the full room. 'Only the hotel,' he told her huskily. 'I have no intention of leaving Selchurch without you.'

Keilly flushed, looking about them self-consciously, aware that his identity had started to become obvious to others in the room, an interested silence beginning to fall in their immediate vicinity. 'And I never intend to leave,' she turned back to him with angry eyes.

'Selchurch is a nice little town, with even nicer people,' he added pointedly. 'But you can't stay here for the rest of your life.'

'Why not, plenty of other people do,' she returned tightly.

'Not you, Keilly,' he said confidently.

'I seem to remember your telling me I belonged here,' she scorned. 'Or was that just part of your routine?'

His eyes hardened at the taunt, his jaw tightening. 'You do belong to the sea, with all its moods,' he bit out. 'But this is far from the only sea in the world. You've met the challenge here, Keilly, it's time to move on.'

'With you?'

Rod drew in a controlling breath at her derision. 'Yes,' he finally answered.

'No, thank you,' she looked at him with narrowed eyes. 'And if you're no longer staying at the hotel where are you living?'

He looked as if he would prefer to pursue the subject of her leaving Selchurch with him some more, but the stubborn set to her jaw told him it would do no good at the moment. 'I'm renting a cottage outside the town. The hotel was very comfortable, but I need a little more privacy than it can provide. Especially with the Easter season coming up.'

Keilly gave him a sharp look; Easter was weeks away! 'Won't you be gone by then? The Oscars——'

'Are after Easter,' he seemed pleased she had remembered. 'I'm not leaving without you, Keilly,' he repeated firmly.

Her mouth twisted. 'I can guarantee that you will.'

'Not without a fight,' he met her challenge.

They had been talking in hushed voices during the exchange, although Keilly knew the fact that they were talking at all was still causing a lot of speculation; she had no intention of adding to that speculation by openly arguing with him.

'You'll get your fight,' she warned vehemently. 'Now if you'll excuse me, I have to——' she broke off with something like panic. As she had turned to leave she had caught the waving hand of acknowledgement from across the room, Kathy even now weaving her way through the crowd towards them, ignorant as to the identity of Keilly's companion, she felt sure!

Kathy had wondered if she had changed over the last ten years, now Keilly found herself wondering if Rod had. The lines of cynicism and experience about his eyes couldn't have been present in the twenty-one-year-old man, and she doubted his body had been quite so masculinely filled out either. The style of his hair would have been longer too then, and although it grew darkly over his collar now she knew it must have been much longer ten years ago. Kathy certainly hadn't recognised him on sight anyway!

'Keilly, I——' Kathy's shocked blue eyes widened in

horror as she finally reached them, all colour leaving her face as she stared at Rod Bartlett.

Keilly was watching for his reaction, and for a brief moment she saw something like puzzled recognition flicker in his eyes before it was replaced by polite interest. In that moment she knew he had no idea who Kathy was. She was elated for her cousin's sake, disappointed that he really was the type of man who slept with a woman and just as easily forgot her.

She suddenly realised that if anyone were to save this situation it would have to be her, Rod was unaware that there *was* a situation, and Kathy was too shocked to do anything more than gape at the man she had dreaded meeting again.

'Kathy,' she put her arm through her cousin's, effectively making them a team against the man who looked at them with questioning eyes. 'This is Rod Bartlett,' she introduced brightly, her hand on Kathy's arm urging her to relax a little. 'Mr Bartlett, this is Mrs Kathy Carmichael, a very good friend of mine.'

Kathy looked at her sharply for her mode of introduction, and with a silent pleading in her eyes Keilly willed her cousin to understand what she was trying to hide. She squeezed her arm in an effort to make her realise she was omitting the fact that they were cousins, that Kathy's name had once been Grant too.

'Er—Hello, Mr Bartlett,' Kathy at last managed to speak. 'You'll have to forgive me,' she managed to sound rueful. 'I had heard you were in Selchurch, but it's a little overwhelming to actually meet you. How do you like being back?' She held out her hand politely.

Keilly was so proud of her in that moment that she could almost have hugged her right there and then. Rod may be the actor but Kathy was giving a wonderful performance!

'I like it very much,' Rod assured her. 'And I can assure you the pleasure in meeting you is all mine.'

Kathy looked a little disconcerted by the way he held on to her hand a little too long, releasing herself with effort. 'I actually came over to ask if you would mind helping me with the teas for a few minutes?' she spoke to Keilly, pleading in her troubled blue eyes. 'As usual I've been let down with my helpers. You wouldn't mind, Mr Bartlett?'

'I——'

'I'm sure Mr Bartlett has other people to meet and talk to,' she firmly interrupted him. 'Perhaps I'll see you again later,' she dismissed, giving him a saccharin-sweet smile.

'Keilly!'

She moistened her lips as she turned back to face him, Kathy fast disappearing back to the kitchen among the crowd. 'Yes?' She released her arm from his grasp.

Rod compelled her to look up at him with the quiet intensity of his gaze. 'You *will* see me later,' he told her softly.

It was a warning, she knew that. Damn the man, why couldn't he just go and leave them all in peace? But she knew the answer to that already, knew that he was staying because he wanted her, because he had the time and inclination to pursue her until he was sure she would give in. And all the time he was here Kathy would fear recognition. What a tangle it all was.

'Keilly, how good to see you again,' called an enthusiastic voice that she recognised as belonging to the youngest son of their local doctor.

'Michael,' she greeted him more warmly than usual, grateful for his timely interruption of a situation she just didn't know how to cope with. She had been out with

Michael on a casual basis several times in the past, although his charming manner and blond good looks did little more than make her feel relaxed in his company. 'How lovely to see you here. Excuse me,' she told Rod in a preoccupied voice, walking away to join Michael, sure that Rod would make no more of a scene here. He had made his warning, he knew it was enough. 'How are you, Michael?' she smiled up at him encouragingly, aware of deep blue eyes boring a hole into her back.

'All the better for seeing you,' he was pleased by her warmth. 'It's been too long,' he smiled down at her.

'Only a few weeks,' she gave him a bright smile. 'Look, I have to go and help Kathy out in the kitchen,' she excused herself, looking across the room to find Rod now surrounded by a group of ecstatic fans. No doubt he was revelling in the recognition, egotistical man that he was! 'It really was lovely to see you again.'

He looked disappointed. 'But, Keilly, I—When can I see you again?' he delayed her.

She really had no wish to encourage him, knowing from experience that he could be a little intense. But if Rod Bartlett thought she was already involved with another man he may be a little less insistent in his own pursuit of her. She was desperate enough to try anything! 'How about tonight?' she suggested decisively. 'I should be able to get away by about eight.'

'Eight o'clock sounds good,' he agreed enthusiastically.

Kathy was on her own when Keilly finally reached the kitchen, and from the look of the queue waiting for their tea she wasn't coping very well. Keilly took over with cool efficiency, her usually unflappable cousin actually shaking by the time they were once again alone.

'What on earth is *he* doing here?' she groaned, the

strain about her eyes having increased during the last few minutes.

'The same as everyone else,' Keilly shrugged. 'Looking round.'

'At a local bazaar!'

She knew Rod had come here for the sole purpose of seeing her, and she blushed guiltily.

'You have to get rid of him, Keilly,' her cousin raised a shaking hand to her brow.

'How?' she sighed.

'I don't know,' Kathy shook her head. 'I couldn't believe it when I saw him just standing there, as if he's been coming to small-town functions like this all his life!'

Keilly knew exactly how her cousin felt, she had been stunned herself. 'He probably did when he was younger,' she reminded. 'After all, he did live here until he was eighteen.'

'He has to go,' Kathy said shakily. 'He just has to go!'

'We can't make him leave,' she pointed out gently.

'Well he can't stay here!' Kathy was on the verge of tears. 'I can't keep running into him like this, I'll be a nervous wreck!'

'But he didn't recognise you——'

'Maybe not this time, maybe not even the next time, but one of these days he just might,' she shuddered at the thought.

'What could he do if he does remember you?' Keilly reasoned.

'You can ask that?' Kathy trembled.

'He's hardly likely to go out and broadcast it in the street that the two of you once slept together——'

'If just one person should find out . . .! You know what the gossip is like in a small place like this,' she groaned. 'One person could know at lunchtime and by the evening the whole town would know! You should realise that better than most, Keilly—Oh God, what have I said now!' she groaned as she saw Keilly pale. 'I didn't mean it like that, love,' she touched Keilly's arm pleadingly. 'Keilly, please! I'm just in a panic, I don't know what I'm saying.'

But it had been said now. She could forget it for weeks at a time now she was older, wouldn't allow it to bother her even when she did think of it. It was only when someone close to her, someone she cared about made such remarks that she remembered the taunting she had taken as a child, the misery of being the teenage daughter of a woman who hadn't married her child's father. It was considered a woman's right nowadays, her choice whether to marry the father, or indeed whether to keep the baby either, but over twenty years ago it still had the stigma of illegitimacy attached to it, the natural assumption that it had been the father who rejected his responsibility. And maybe her father had, her mother had never discussed him or his identity with her, leaving Keilly with a questioning shadow in her life that would never be answered.

It was the reason she rarely dated, of course, the reason she had been so shocked by her behaviour with Rod on the beach that night, the reason she had felt so betrayed when she knew how he had deceived her, the reason she found his seduction of Kathy so unacceptable. As a vulnerable teenager without a father or mother too many boys had lied to her believing, because of her fatherless background, that she would accept the brief warmth and love they had so 'generously' offered. Rod Bartlett had been no better; she already knew he would lie to get what he wanted!

It was her gratitude to her mother's brother and

sister-in-law for the way they had always stood by her and her mother that made Keilly so loyal to them and the cousin that had become like a true sister to her. It was also because of the shame her mother had been made to feel by other people that she was so determined Kathy should not be put in the middle of such a crisis.

'It doesn't matter,' she dismissed, although she knew that it did. The origin of her birth would always matter to her, which was another reason she despised Rod Bartlett's life-style. 'You just have to calm down, Kathy. If anyone should see you like this . . .!'

Her warning had the desired effect: Kathy regaining her composure. 'You're right,' she said in a controlled voice. 'I'll be all right now,' she smoothed the silky skirt of the dress she wore as she prepared to take care of the refreshments once again. 'I'll be fine,' she assured Keilly.

And Kathy did seem to have regained her equilibrium as she smiled her way through the rest of the afternoon. Although that might have had something to do with the fact that Rod Bartlett left after only half an hour, making a polite if firm exit from the fans who crowded around him interestedly.

They probably wondered why he was slumming too, Keilly thought unfairly. If only they knew he was pursuing the daughter of Estelle Grant, the woman who had caused so much of a scandal herself twenty-two years ago!

It was just her luck that they had to be busy that evening and Brenda was off sick. When Michael arrived she had to ask him if he would rather cancel their date or wait in the bar for her until about ten-thirty when she would have finished serving the meals. He had chosen to wait, although between running to the kitchen and serving she didn't have a lot of time to talk to him.

She knew the minute Rod Bartlett came into the hotel, knew it by the tingle of awareness down her spine. She turned to see him coming in from the blustery weather outside, wearing the sheepskin jacket of their first meeting to keep out the January wind.

'Keilly, I want to talk to you,' he warned as she turned away, his eyes narrowed.

Her mouth twisted as she turned back to him with rebellious eyes. 'As you can see, I'm busy,' she looked down pointedly at the plates she was returning to the kitchen.

He frowned. 'No Brenda tonight?'

The other girl would have been thrilled that he had remembered her name! 'Obviously not,' she derided.

'Okay,' he nodded. 'I'll wait in the bar until you've finished.'

Where he would obviously see Michael. After her warmth to Michael this afternoon he was sure to put two and two together and come up with the right conclusion; that Michael was waiting for her too. For a girl that didn't date very often she was lining them up tonight! 'If that's what you want to do,' she agreed lightly.

'I do,' Rod said firmly.

'Please yourself,' she shrugged, smiling to herself as she went into the kitchen.

When she came back to the dining room to find Rod seated alone at one of the tables she knew he had indeed added two and two together, and from the dark scowl on his face he didn't like the conclusion he had come to at all!

He had the menu open in front of him as she went over to take his order, although he didn't appear to be interested in choosing anything.

'Is young Fenwick waiting for you?' he bit out tautly.

'He's twenty-four,' she scorned the 'young' Fenwick. 'And how do you know who he is?'

'I was at school with his elder brother,' Rod dismissed tersely.

'I should have known!' She pulled a face. 'Now would you like something to eat, I'm afraid it's almost time to stop taking orders,' she added without a shred of regret.

'I only want a dessert and coffee——'

'This isn't a coffee shop, Mr Bartlett,' she flashed.

He looked up at her with calm eyes. 'I'm sure your aunt wouldn't refuse a recent ex-guest a little sustenance. Dessert and coffee are all I can manage.'

'Why?'

'Use your imagination,' he taunted.

'You've already eaten,' she sighed.

'Quite adequately,' he nodded. 'I can cook myself a meal if the need arises.'

'Then why eat again?' she demanded impatiently.

'So that I can see you, of course,' he was perfectly relaxed as he sat back in the chair, the black roll-neck sweater fitting smoothly to his muscular chest and shoulders, the black corduroys moulded to the lean length of his long legs.

'You've seen me,' she looked down at him defiantly, seeing everything in him that must have been in her father, all the selfishness he must once have shown her mother, that Rod would show her given the chance. 'There's no need to go to the bother of having dessert and coffee.'

'It's no bother,' he drawled challengingly. 'You didn't answer my question, is Fenwick waiting for you?'

'Yes,' she avoided the steel of his eyes. 'He's a friend of mine, he has been for some time.'

Rod's hand clamped about her wrist as she would have moved away. 'How much of a friend?' he demanded to know.

'Just a friend,' she repeated tautly.

'Then he won't mind you coming out to dinner with me tomorrow night, will he.'

'He might not,' she moved pointedly away from him. 'But I would. If you'll excuse me, Mr Bartlett, I have other, more genuine, customers to serve.'

He looked pointedly at the last couple still in the dining room besides himself, quirking dark brows as they exited, leaving them completely alone. 'There appears to be—only me.'

'And you're merely wasting my time,' she snapped.

His expression hardened. 'I'll have some of your aunt's delicious cheesecake. And coffee, of course.'

Her mouth set angrily but she went off to get the pie and coffee anyway; her aunt had *never* turned a customer away, no matter how little they chose to eat.

'Thank you,' Rod taunted her as she brought back his order. 'I'm sure Fenwick won't mind waiting for you.'

She gave a sarcastically sweet smile. 'I'm sure he won't.'

'Talking of your friends,' he said slowly, savouring the cherry cheesecake. 'Your friend of this afternoon seemed, familiar.'

The coffee pot shook precariously in her hand. 'Which friend was that?' Her mouth suddenly felt dry.

He seemed to think for a moment. 'Mrs Carmichael, I think you called her. The pretty blonde woman doing the teas,' he supplied by way of explanation, looking up enquiringly. 'I have the feeling I've met her before.'

Keilly's tongue felt cleaved to the roof of her mouth. 'You used to live here, I'm sure a lot of people are going to seem familiar,' she was finally able to speak. Could he possibly remember Kathy, after *ten* years?

'Maybe,' but he didn't sound convinced.

'Maybe you were at school with her too,' she suggested quickly. 'You're probably of a similar age group.'

'Maybe,' he said again, finishing off his cheesecake with some relish. 'I'm sure it will come back to me where we've met before. I'll give it some thought.'

Unless he had something else, something he wanted more badly, on his mind. 'Where were you thinking of going tomorrow night?' she asked with a casualness she was far from feeling. The last thing she wanted was to leave herself open to the brand of seduction this man exercised, a brand of seduction she had already succumbed to more than once. But she had to take his mind off Kathy—any way that she could!

He looked surprised. 'You'll come?'

She shrugged. 'Depends where you're going.'

'Anywhere you want to go,' he said instantly.

'I——'

'Keilly, are—Oh, sorry,' Michael stood awkwardly in the doorway. 'Your uncle thought you had finished for the evening.'

'She has,' Rod stood up decisively, pulling on his coat with unhurried movements, leaving the money for his order on the table. 'Say hello to your brother for me, Michael,' he spoke smoothly to the other man, walking to the door.

'Oh but—er—Rod?' Keilly halted him, very self-conscious in front of the other man. 'What about tomorrow night?' she mumbled.

'Tomorrow . . .?' for a moment he looked puzzled, then his brow cleared. 'I'll call you,' he nodded. 'I've already delayed you long enough tonight.' He gave

Michael a wide smile. 'I hope I haven't fouled up your evening too badly.'

'Er—no,' Michael seemed confused by their conversation. 'We were only going to have a drink together anyway, and there's still time for that.'

'Good,' Rod nodded, turning to look at Keilly with enigmatic eyes. 'Please tell your aunt how much I enjoyed the cheesecake.' With a brief impersonal nod that encompassed them both, he left.

Keilly stared after him with frustrated anger. He had come to the hotel purposely to see her, had eaten food he didn't really want for the same reason, and yet as soon as she had agreed to see him tomorrow he had lost interest. What game was he playing with her—and why?

'Ready, Keilly?'

She turned with a start, having forgotten Michael was there at all. 'I'll—er—I'll just tidy away here,' she said jerkily. 'And join you in the bar in five minutes.'

She wasn't very good company for him for what remained of the evening, she knew she wasn't, and yet there was nothing she could do about it, her thoughts were preoccupied. Why had Rod suddenly lost interest like that? Surely he couldn't just have been testing that she was still attracted to him despite her date with Michael? That didn't sound like him at all. And yet what did she really know of him, except that he could lie and cheat to achieve his objective. Had her capitulation tonight been enough for him, would he move on to a new quarry now?

CHAPTER FIVE

KEILLY woke with a mouth that felt as if it were coated with sandpaper and a dull throb in her temples. It was the first time she had ever had a hangover in her life, but after the five vodka and limes she had consumed with startling rapidity she thought she probably deserved it!

Her evening with Michael had not been a success. She had been tense and confused, and his brief goodnight kiss had done little to banish the thought of other, more experienced, lips as they moved over hers. After Michael had left she had gone back to the bar and had another drink with her uncle, loath to go up to her bedroom yet, wary of thoughts of Rod, of how much she really wanted to see him the following evening, and not just for Kathy's sake. Considering her own fatherless background, she knew she was taking a risk being attracted to such a man, and yet she couldn't seem to help it.

But she needn't have worried about thoughts of Rod once she got to bed, the unaccustomed drink had taken its toll and she had fallen into a dream-filled sleep. A quick glance at the bedroom clock showed her that it was already after eight, that she had been asleep for almost nine hours, and yet she didn't feel rested, startled into complete wakefulness as the telephone on her bedside table began to ring. Probably her aunt wondering why she wasn't down to breakfast yet. Just the thought of food right now made her feel ill!

'Yes?' she managed to articulate into the mouthpiece.

'Keilly?'

Even over the telephone Rod's voice managed to sound smooth and melodious. 'Yes,' she managed again.

'You sound awful,' he questioned. 'Don't you feel well?'

'I feel fine,' she moaned. 'It's these little men with their hammers I'm worried about,' she grimaced as she tried to sit up, the pounding in her head becoming worse. 'They can't seem to get out of my head,' she added weakly.

Rod gave a throaty chuckle. 'I would imagine seeing you sozzled is quite something.'

'Not the morning after it isn't.' She leant back against the pillows she had propped up behind her. 'What can I do for you, Mr Bartlett?' she asked briskly deciding there had been enough pleasantries between them for now.

'You can tell me what time Fenwick left you last night,' he grated.

Colour flooded her cheeks at the erroneous assumption he had made. 'About an hour after you did,' she snapped. 'Now if that's all you called for——'

'It isn't,' he said quickly. 'I'll pick you up at seven-thirty tonight, all right?'

'Do I have a choice?' she mumbled.

'I don't recall having to use force to make you accept my invitation,' he said icily.

No, he hadn't forced her, but circumstances had. If she wanted to help Kathy she had no choice. 'Seven-thirty will be fine,' she agreed stiltedly. 'Now if you don't mind I'd like to go and take something to stop the little men with their hammers.'

Rod gave another laugh of enjoyment. 'I wish you luck.' He rang off abruptly.

It was a miracle how she managed to get through the day, although she knew it was partly due to the cups of coffee she consumed. Michael telephoned to see how she was, and she turned down his invitation for tomorrow, knowing now that the thought of her already having a boyfriend hadn't put Rod off at all.

Going out for a meal was the last thing she felt like in the circumstances, and yet she obediently went up to her room at seven o'clock to get ready for her date, the black and grey velvet dress warm against the brisk January winds, with a high button collar, grey lace yoke and cuffs, the style loose and comfortable, although nevertheless managing to complement the perfection of her figure.

Rod's eyes darkened appreciatively as she joined him downstairs, and it was only with tremendous effort of will she was able to withstand the brief kiss he caressed across her parted lips. He looked devastating, the black dinner jacket and snowy white shirt fitting him perfectly, his hair lightly tousled by the breeze.

'You look beautiful,' he told her huskily, taking her elbow to guide her out to his waiting car.

She resisted the impulse to tell him he did too, although it would have been no less than the truth. She had never seen such a handsome man, his skin lightly tanned except for the lighter colour of his jaw where his beard had been shaved off. It was this fact that reminded her how he had deceived her when he came here two months ago, and it would remain a visual reminder of how stupid she had been to trust him then.

'For you,' he handed her a small cellophane-wrapped box before turning to start the engine of the Jaguar.

She looked down wordlessly at the single red rose against the bed of black velvet, feeling something twist in her heart. How many other woman had received this seemingly romantic gesture in the past, had Kathy known it too? Perhaps not, Rod had been a little poorer then, no more than a student himself, and so probably unable to afford such luxuries to seduce his women. But no doubt dozens of women had received a similar red rose from him since then.

'Thank you,' she said stiltedly, putting the box down on the console between them. 'It's beautiful,' she added woodenly, without any real warmth.

Rod gave her a puzzled sideways glance, driving the Jaguar with speed and efficiency of movement. 'Won't you wear it on your gown?' he suggested softly.

'It seems a pity to take it out of the box,' she refused. 'It looks so nice there. Where are we going?' she changed the subject.

'The steak house on the other side of town,' he told her in a dismissive tone. 'How are the little men with their hammers this evening?'

'Taking a rest,' she said abruptly. 'Did you book a table at the restaurant, it can get very busy?'

'I booked a table,' he nodded.

'Although I don't suppose you usually have trouble getting a table, anywhere, do you,' she realised derisively.

His hands tightened briefly on the steering-wheel. 'Not usually, no,' he acknowledged tautly.

'Oh to be rich and famous,' she mocked.

'I'm not as rich as you might think,' he bit out. 'The roles I take don't always pay well, but I'd rather do something I believe in than something that just pays well. As for being famous,' his mouth twisted, 'that can definitely have its drawbacks.'

Keilly quickly discovered that one of them was being stared at in restaurants! Most of the other diners were too polite to actually come over and speak to Rod, although one or two did, and he always reacted courteously. But even if people didn't actually come over and speak to him they stared at him constantly. Rod seemed immune to their stares, although their constant attention to their every movement was starting to grate on Keilly's nerves.

'Doesn't it bother you?' she finally had to ask him.

'Being looked at?' He instantly knew what was worrying her. 'Yes, it bothers me. And when I'm in London I try to avoid situations like this as much as possible. But I didn't think you would have agreed to going back to my cottage for a meal,' he added dryly.

'No,' she confirmed.

'And eating at the hotel would hardly be taking you out,' he shrugged.

She could see what point he was trying to make, but this was like being in a goldfish bowl! 'I couldn't stand this all the time,' she sipped her coffee with relief, glad the meal was over and they could soon leave.

'I'm sorry, Keilly,' he put his hand over hers. 'I didn't realise it would upset you as much as it is.'

She quickly released her hand from his, aware of the instant increase of conversation about them even if he wasn't. Rod couldn't understand the torment of a fatherless childhood that had given her a need to stay out of the limelight as much as possible, never to draw undue attention to herself. Most actors were known to thrive on such adulation, how could he possibly understand how she felt about it?

'It isn't usually this bad, believe me,' he assured her at her continued silence. 'There are lots of places in London where you're totally ignored.'

She held back a shudder with effort, no longer willing to raise her gaze from the table-top. 'This isn't London,' she reminded him stiffly.

EXTRA BONUS
MAIL YOUR ORDER
TODAY AND GET A
FREE TOTE BAG
FROM HARLEQUIN.

Business Reply Mail
No Postage Stamp
Necessary if Mailed
in Canada

Postage will be paid by

Harlequin Reader Service
P.O. Box 2800
5170 Yonge Street
Postal Station A
Willowdale, Ontario
M2N 9Z9

'No,' he acknowledged heavily, concern for her in his troubled blue eyes. 'Hell, this isn't the way I wanted it to be at all,' he rasped. 'I wanted you to enjoy this evening, for us to finally get to know each other in a relaxed atmosphere. You really hate this recognition, don't you?'

'Yes!'

'Would you like to leave?'

'More than anything,' she nodded quickly.

'Then we will,' he sighed, signalling the waitress for their bill.

Keilly was still shaking with reaction when they got outside to the car park, raising no objection when Rod took her in his arms, holding her comfortingly against his chest. She needed his warmth at the moment, felt badly shaken by what had happened in the restaurant.

'It's still early, come back to the cottage with me?' Rod urged against her temple.

The cottage offered privacy after what had been nothing more than a public spectacle. She nodded in silent agreement, letting him help her into the car, huddling down into her woollen coat until he got the heating working.

'You'll soon warm up,' he assured her, giving her a concerned glance.

It wasn't only the weather that made her feel chilled, although she couldn't tell him that. How could she suffer through more evenings like tonight, even for Kathy's sake?

Rod was as silent as she on the drive to the cottage he was renting, and she was glad of these few minutes to collect herself. She knew it wasn't only being stared at that had upset her, that the headache from this morning was still with her. Altogether it had been a disastrous day for her.

She knew Selchurch well enough to realise, even in the dark, that the cottage Rod was driving to was actually on Peter's estate! Her mind froze in horror at the thought, although she knew Peter probably didn't even realise, as his manager dealt with the rental of the cottages. She felt certain Kathy had no idea!

'It's quite comfortable,' Rod told her as he opened her door for her before leading the way up the unlit path to the front door, unlocking it to switch on the lights.

Keilly knew just how comfortable these cottages were, knew they had been converted into luxury dwellings from the small estate cottages that used to be rented by the estate workers during Peter's father's day. Peter had built all new houses for his workers, knocking two of these old cottages into one and renting them out during the summer months. If Rod had made enquiries about one any later than April he wouldn't have found one available.

The lounge had retained its beamed ceiling and stone walls, the thick green carpet and brown leather suite all chosen by Kathy to fit in with the character of the cottage, the fireplace the main centre of the room, although the fire was only needed for show nowadays, central heating installed along with the conversions. There was also a large kitchen down here fitted with all the modern conveniences, plus a small dining room, and upstairs would be the three medium-sized bedrooms and the luxurious bathroom. There were ten such cottages on the estate, although this was the remotest of them all, an indication that Rod liked his privacy too—when he could get it. This only managed to remind her of the ordeal she had just suffered, sitting down suddenly in one of the wing-backed leather armchairs.

'Here.'

She looked up to find a glass of what smelt revoltingly like brandy being held out in front of her. 'No, thanks,' she refused with distaste, having drunk only water during their meal in preference to the wine Rod had enjoyed.

'It will help,' he encouraged gently. 'And who knows,' he added mockingly. 'It could help get rid of that hangover you still have.'

Her eyes widened. 'How did you——'

'I've had one or two myself in the past,' he mused.

Her mouth tightened. 'Of course,' she acknowledged as she took the glass and swallowed some of the liquid, instantly beginning to cough.

Rod laughed softly as he patted her on the back. 'Has it taken your mind off your headache?'

She glared up at him. 'Very funny. I think I would prefer coffee.'

He straightened. 'I'll get some,' he nodded, his eyes still glinting with humour as he left the room.

Keilly listened to him moving about the kitchen for a few minutes before getting up to join him. She stood in the doorway watching as he prepared the percolated coffee, the kitchen surprisingly tidy despite the obvious evidence of habitation.

He turned as if aware of her presence, the jacket to his dinner suit despatched to a kitchen chair, the snowy white shirt fitting snugly to his powerful chest and taut stomach, the tie discarded and the top two buttons of his shirt undone. He looked comfortably relaxed, as if he were used to doing things like this for himself. Which brought her back to the question of who Barbie was.

'Do you live alone in London?' she asked the question casually, although she knew by the way his brows went down over his eyes that he had caught the hidden question.

He turned to lean back against the kitchen unit, his eyes narrowed. 'Since Veronica died, yes,' he finally answered.

Her eyes widened. 'You haven't lived with anyone for six years?'

'No,' he bit out, his mouth tight. 'A commitment to live with someone is a big decision, not something I would do lightly. Although that doesn't mean there haven't been women.'

'Of course not,' Keilly derided.

His expression darkened. 'I said there had been women, that doesn't mean I jumped into bed with someone else the day after she died!'

She blushed at his angry rebuke. 'I wasn't implying that you had——'

'Weren't you?' he scorned, carrying the tray of coffee into the lounge, brushing past her with no indication that he knew he had even touched her.

'I really wasn't,' she protested, following him. 'I just wondered who Barbie was,' she admitted tightly.

Rod poured the coffee, waiting for her to be seated opposite him before he answered her. 'Barbie is my secretary.'

'Secretary?' she repeated disbelievingly.

'That's right,' his mouth quirked mockingly. 'The telephone call I received from her the first time I was here was to let me know they had started the location shooting on my last film earlier than scheduled, and that I was expected in California immediately. Barbie keeps me sane by telling me where I should be at any given time, organises my travel and anything else I might ask of her.'

'I see,' Keilly didn't sound convinced.

Rod shook his head, his mouth twisted wryly. 'I don't think you do. Barbie is very happily married to her husband of the last fifteen years, and has three lovely children to show for it. I'm even godfather to the youngest,' he added mockingly. 'Barbie *is* a wife, but not mine.'

'Oh.'

'Suitably chastened?'

She chewed on her inner lip. 'I suppose so,' she admitted grudgingly.

'Good,' he gave a dazzling smile, moving to sit on the side of her chair. 'Now that we have that settled, could we be friends again?'

Friends was something the two of them could never be, but without exposing Kathy's part in his past she couldn't tell him that. And right at this moment she had something more dangerous than Kathy's exposure to deal with! Rod had removed her coffee cup from her hand and was even now making room for himself in the chair beside her.

'I had such plans for us when I came back,' he told her huskily. 'And you've been so distant from me since you found out I was the despised Rod Bartlett.'

No one could accuse her of being distant now! The whole lengths of their bodies were moulded together in the confines of the chair, and Keilly was finding it difficult to breathe with him so close to her. While he sat opposite her in the restaurant, or beside her in a car she could pretend his male magnetism didn't exist, but alone with him like this she found it difficult not to remember the time on the beach when only the storm raging overhead had broken them apart.

'Why did you change your mind about coming out with me tonight?'

His hand was caressing her cheek, making it difficult for her to think at all, yet alone of a viable answer for him; she couldn't admit to the truth. 'Isn't it a woman's prerogative?' she dismissed, wishing he would stop touching her.

His mouth quirked, very close to her now, his breath warming her cheek. 'I never knew one who didn't.'

'And you've known a lot, haven't you,' she scorned.

'Keilly,' his hand was firm on her chin as he turned her to face him. 'I can't relive my life and make it all neat and tidy for you,' he told her quietly. 'I've made mistakes, done things I'm not proud of, but I can't change any of that now. It's gone, and there is nothing I can do about it.'

No, even if he could ever explain his relationship with Veronica, as he had told her he would one day do, he could never change the fact that he had once made love to Kathy and then let her down. She was a fool to be seduced by his closeness now, and yet she couldn't help it . . .

'Oh, Keilly!' His mouth claimed hers fiercely as he pushed her back into the chair, his body hard and possessive on hers.

She was lost again, as she knew she always would be when he touched or kissed her. She should never have been stupid enough to come back to the cottage with him like this, but it was too late now, too late . . .

His hands restlessly roamed the length of her body, not touching her intimately, seeming to wait for some signal from her that he could do so, continuing to kiss her, his tongue probing the edge of her lips. Of its own volition her tongue moved to meet his. It seemed to be what he had been waiting for, groaning deeply in his throat as his body surged into hers.

As his hand closed over her breast she knew she had to stop this, couldn't let things go any further between them if she were to leave here at all tonight. 'Please stop,' she groaned her panic, pushing lightly against his chest as he seemed not to hear her.

The feel of her hands penetrated when her words had not, and he raised his head to look down at her with darkened eyes.

'Please stop,' she repeated as she saw his puzzled expression.

He drew in a controlling breath. 'You're sure that's what you want?'

When he held her like this, the evidence of his passion throbbing against her, she was no longer sure of anything any more. But she had to be, had to remember she was only with him at all to divert his thoughts from Kathy. 'I'm sure,' she said firmly, getting up out of the chair to straighten her hair. 'I'd like to go home now.'

Rod looked up at her with a rueful smile, his hair rakishly disordered. 'It hasn't been a very successful evening, has it.'

'For whom?'

His brows rose at her sarcasm, and he too stood up. 'For you,' he chided gently. 'I'll have to remember in future that you don't like to be among crowds, and that bringing you back here is definitely out,' he added wryly.

Keilly flushed. 'I'm afraid I'm going to be very busy the next few weeks getting the hotel spring-cleaned for the start of the season at Easter. My aunt always likes everywhere to be thoroughly cleaned before we get really busy.'

'But not every night too, surely?'

She flashed him an irritated look. 'For a while, yes.'

'Does that mean I won't be able to see you?' His eyes narrowed.

She didn't like the way he suddenly seemed suspicious, almost as if he suspected her motives for seeing him tonight. 'I'll still get my days off,' she explained. 'Although I'm not sure when they will be,' she added warningly.

He looked thoughtful. 'You can always call me when you're free,' he suggested. 'After all, I'm only here to see you.'

She blushed at his almost accusing tone. 'You must realise I have a job to do, that I'm not on holiday,' she reminded waspishly. 'I didn't ask you to spend your holiday here,' she told him defensively, although she knew that if he had still been just Rick Richards to her that she would have asked her aunt and uncle for a few days off to be with him.

Rod sighed. 'I accept that I can only see you when you have the time off. Despite what you may think of me, I'm not a spoilt "superstar" who believes he can have his own way in everything. You mean a lot to me, interest me more than any other woman ever has. I haven't even looked at anyone else since I met you.'

'Is that a record?' she mocked.

'No,' he answered her seriously. 'It took me over a year to be attracted to someone else after Veronica died.'

She felt his rebuke. 'I'm sorry,' she murmured, knowing by the deep sincerity in his voice that he meant every word he said, that he had genuinely cared for the other woman.

'Yes,' he dismissed abruptly. 'I'll take you home now.'

'The tray——'

'Leave it,' he instructed curtly.

His quietly controlled anger made her want to apologise yet again, more sincerely this time, until he actually believed she meant what she said. But she couldn't do it, didn't want to be friends with this man when he only had to kiss her to make her forget anything but the two of them.

The drive to the hotel was made in silence, Rod seeming deep in thought, Keilly loath to speak in case she should give in to the temptation to see him again. She had no reason to feel guilty, damn it, especially not guilty enough to foolishly agree to seeing him again.

'I'll see you inside,' he told her once they reached the hotel.

'There's no need——'

'There's every need,' he told her grimly. 'It's late, it's dark, and I intend seeing you into your home.'

When he put it like that she knew she couldn't argue with him any more, picking up the box containing the rose that she had discarded so callously earlier in the evening. It was just her luck that her uncle should be locking up for the night when they reached the door, greeting them both jovially.

'Like a nightcap?' he offered, locking the bar, the hotel curiously silent and empty this time of night.

Keilly inwardly willed Rod to say no, but she knew before he agreed that he was going to accept, the two of them following her uncle into the large homely lounge through the door marked 'Private'. Her aunt, seeing there were two more for the habitual late-night pot of coffee, hurried back to the kitchen to get more cups.

'Did you have a good evening?' she asked them as she poured the hot brew.

'It wasn't a complete success,' Rod was the one to answer her. 'I'm afraid Keilly was subjected to the recognition I've learnt to live with over the past few years.'

'Oh dear,' her aunt gave her a worried look, knowing how Keilly felt about having attention drawn to her. 'That was a pity.'

'Yes,' he agreed softly.

'But if you will go making excellent films . . .' Keilly's uncle teased.

Rod turned to him interestedly. 'Don't tell me that you, unlike your niece, have actually seen some of my films?'

'Quite a few,' her uncle confirmed—much to Keilly's amazement. She had no idea they had seen any of Rod Bartlett's films! They seemed to have liked them too. 'Sylvie and I often sneak off to the cinema for the evening in the winter. "Beginning Again" is due to be at the local cinema any day now.'

'Really?' Rod's eyes narrowed.

'I saw a preview of it on television,' her aunt spoke again. 'It looks very good.'

'I was pleased with it,' he nodded.

She hadn't realised her aunt and uncle were actually fans of his, they had never mentioned it before. Maybe they hadn't liked to after that blistering letter she had written to the magazine!

'Would you like to come to dinner on Saturday, Rod?' she heard her aunt asking him, with some dismay. 'Because we're so busy right through the summer we don't have the time to invite our friends over, so we usually like to have everyone over before the season really gets under way. It will only be a few close friends,' she encouraged. 'And I can assure you they won't all stare at you through the evening,' she smiled.

Keilly looked at Rod with horror in her eyes, wanting him to refuse. After all, what possible interest could he have in her aunt and uncle's dinner party! The answer to that was all too obvious.

'I'd like that very much,' he predictably accepted.

'Good,' her aunt smiled, standing up. 'Bill and I might as well take our coffee upstairs. Saturday at eight o'clock, then, Rod.'

'I'll look forward to it,' he stood up politely as the middle-aged couple left the room.

Keilly was once again lost in her own misery, barely noticing as Rod joined her on the sofa. The dinner party before the start of the holiday season had been a tradition with her aunt and uncle for years, and Kathy and Peter had been coming to them for the last nine!

'You're very quiet,' Rod prompted huskily beside her. 'Would you rather I hadn't accepted your aunt's invitation?' he asked shrewdly.

She gave him a sharp look. 'Of course not. I just— Wouldn't you rather have spent the evening alone with me?'

His eyes darkened in colour, his arm coming about her shoulders. 'You know I would, but tonight didn't work out too well. I thought maybe you would feel more relaxed among friends.'

She probably would have done if Kathy and Peter weren't going to be there!

'Besides,' he added. 'I've accepted now.'

'Yes,' she said dully.

'Hey,' his finger under her chin turned her to face him, his mouth curved into a sensual smile. 'I promise I won't embarrass you,' he chided mockingly.

Colour entered her cheeks. 'I didn't think you would,' she snapped. 'It's just that——'

'It will be all right Keilly,' his thumbtip on her lips prevented further speech. 'Now walk me to the door and I'll see you on Saturday.'

'Rod, I'm really sorry about what I said earlier,' she told him when they reached the door. 'I didn't realise how—sensitive you still are about—about Veronica.'

'I know,' he looked down at her with warm eyes. 'But she did mean a lot to me. Can you really not see me until Saturday?' His gaze was sensual on her parted lips.

She probably could if she wanted to, her aunt didn't make her work twenty-four hours a day, but she didn't think she wanted to. 'No,' she answered firmly.

'Then this will have to sustain me until then,' he murmured, bending his head to part her lips with his, drawing her into him, his hands on her spine curving her body against his, drinking his fill of her until he felt her tremble in his arms. 'Keilly, Keilly,' he muttered against her temple. 'If you only knew how much you mean to me——'

'Rod, please——'

'It's all right, darling,' he soothed as he sensed her panic. 'I'm not about to ruin things again by moving too fast for you. Although by Saturday I'm likely to be climbing the walls for you,' he added ruefully, chuckling softly at her blushingly outraged expression. 'Have pity, Keilly, all I can do right now is talk about it.' He kissed her lingeringly on the temple. 'Pleasant dreams, my darling. I'll be looking forward to Saturday.'

She stood at the door and watched until the tail-lights of the Jaguar disappeared into the distance, all the time wondering how she was going to break this particular piece of news to Kathy. It wasn't going to be easy!

CHAPTER SIX

'WHAT on earth can my mother have been thinking of?' Kathy glanced worriedly at the door for about the tenth time since her arrival a few minutes earlier. 'Why on earth did she have to invite *him* here tonight?'

As she had known she would her cousin had taken the news of Rod's expected presence at the dinner party with a mixture of horror and fatalism, sure that tonight her past association with him would come out.

'I tried every way I could think of to get out of coming here this evening,' Kathy continued tautly. 'I pretended a headache, sickness, that Heather's cold seemed to be coming back. Peter just shrugged them all off,' she trembled. 'I feel like a prisoner waiting for the executioner!' she added with a groan.

Most of the guests had already arrived for dinner, although Rod was still noticeably absent. She had no doubt that he would be here though, had seen him at the hotel bar on several evenings the past week, and he had given no indication then that he didn't intend coming tonight. But it was already eight-fifteen, her aunt would be serving dinner soon, with or without Rod.

'Do you have any idea what could be delaying Mr Bartlett?' her aunt appeared at her side, calm and unruffled, used to coping when it came to cooking meals.

'None at all,' Keilly answered truthfully.

'I see,' her aunt turned back to the kitchen. 'Well if he doesn't arrive soon we shall have to start without him;

otherwise everyone is going to be drunk before we have our meal,' she derided the liberally flowing alcohol.

'She's lucky it's only dinner she has to worry about,' Kathy muttered once she and Keilly were alone again. 'What can be keeping the man?'

Keilly wondered that too; he had proven his punctuality in the past, so it really wasn't like him to be late. It was totally incomprehensible to her, but she was actually getting worried about him! She looked at her watch once more, twenty past eight. Something must surely be wrong.

'I won't be long,' she told Kathy quickly, moving towards the door.

'Where are you going?' her cousin frowned her puzzlement.

'To telephone Rod,' she explained impatiently. 'Isn't it obvious?'

Kathy caught hold of her arm as they emerged into the reception area, the restaurant closed for this one evening of the year, and a couple of local men running the bar for her uncle. 'Are you mad?' Kathy demanded incredulously, her voice soft, conscious of where they were. 'What more could we ask for than him not turning up?' She looked at Keilly as if she had lost her senses.

'He could be hurt——'

'More than likely he's decided the evening will be too tame for him——'

'Kathy!' she turned on her cousin angrily—something she couldn't ever remember doing before. 'Will you just, for once, stop thinking of yourself,' she snapped, uncaring of Kathy's indignant expression. 'He meant to be here tonight, so there must be a good reason why he isn't.'

Kathy looked angry—her nostrils flared. 'It couldn't

just be that he's lost interest in you, could it?' she scorned nastily.

The comment didn't deserve an answer and Keilly didn't offer one, going over to the telephone and dialling the number of the cottage, watching dispassionately as Kathy spun on her heel and re-entered the lounge, her expression stormy.

The receiver wasn't picked up at the cottage, which meant Rod was either not there or else he was unable to come to the telephone. The thought of the latter made her tremble, and she knew in that moment that no matter what Rod had done in the past, what cruelty he had inflicted, she had fallen in love with him. Despite all the odds, her own common sense, she knew she had done the unforgivable and fallen in love with him. The thought of him perhaps being injured and unable to call for help horrified her, and she knew that for her own peace of mind she had to go to the cottage and see if he was all right.

'Take my car, love,' her uncle gave her his keys once she had explained what she was doing. 'It will be better for getting down the track that leads to the cottage.'

Her long grey-blue gown was hardly suitable for driving, but she had no time to go and change, not if she wasn't to delay her aunt's dinner too much longer. The roads were wet from yet another downpour, which made the going slower than she would have wished, and it was with some relief that she finally reached the rough road that led to the cottage. The parked Jaguar almost at the top of the track, noticeably minus its driver, didn't reassure her in the least. Where was Rod?

The Jaguar blocking the driveway meant she couldn't drive down to the cottage, and leaving the car parked on the road she walked down the tarmaced pathway, relieved when she saw most of the lights were on in the cottage. But if Rod was there why hadn't he answered the telephone?

'Darling!' He answered the door as soon as he heard her knock, pulling her quickly inside the warmth of the cottage, holding her tightly in his arms.

It took her a few minutes to realise he was wearing only a towel draped around his waist, his torso and long legs completely bare, his hair still damp from the shower he seemed to have taken.

She pulled out of his arms, looking at him accusingly. 'You really weren't coming to the dinner party!' she realised heatedly. 'I thought you were ill or injured, but you just weren't coming! It would have been polite to call my aunt——'

'I did call her,' he said quietly, hitching the towel more securely about his hips.

'Don't lie to me on top of everything else,' she snapped. 'You——'

'I called your aunt ten minutes ago, as soon as I got back to the cottage.'

'From where?' she demanded to know.

'From the driveway,' he told her gently. 'You can't have missed my car parked almost at the top?'

'No. But——'

'That was as far as I managed to push it before I fell flat on my face in the mud,' he continued dryly, his dark brows arched mockingly at her disbelieving expression.

'You—fell . . .'

'Flat on my face,' he nodded. 'My car got stuck in the mud next to the cottage; after all the rain we've had I shouldn't have been surprised! I managed to drive it a little way and then it just wouldn't move any further. Pushing it seemed like a good idea at the time,' he grimaced. 'But not quite so good when I slipped and landed in the mud.'

Keilly had been having difficulty in keeping a straight face while he gave his explanation, the last was just too much for her, her eyes dancing with mischief as she began to laugh. 'I'd love to have seen it,' she began to giggle. 'Oh, Rod, how funny!'

'Very,' he drawled. 'I telephoned the hotel as soon as I got back and your aunt told me you were coming out here. It's taken me all this time to wash the mud off me. Now are you going to stop laughing,' he was advancing on her menacingly. 'Or am I going to have to make you?'

She sobered as suddenly as she had started laughing. 'I didn't mean——'

'Not quick enough,' he growled as he took her into his arms.

'My aunt is waiting for us——'

'A few more minutes isn't going to make much difference now. Besides,' he murmured against her throat. 'Your aunt told me not to rush.'

With the recent discovery of her love for him she had no defence against his kisses, melting against him, her arms up about his neck as she kissed him back, parting her lips to allow him access to all the dark recesses of her mouth.

'God, Keilly,' he groaned raggedly as he lifted his head slightly. 'Why couldn't you have been like this when we didn't have to hurry off?'

She smiled. 'Maybe for that very reason.'

His own smile was rueful. 'At least you're honest.' He smoothed back the darkness of her hair. 'We have months to get to know each other, I'm not going to rush you. But after being kissed like that I'm not going to let you see Fenwick again either,' he added with a hardening of his eyes.

'I told you, he's just a friend.' The feel of his bare

torso beneath her hands was making her breathless and in that moment she knew she didn't care who he was, or that her aunt and uncle were waiting for them. In that moment she wanted him so badly none of it mattered. 'Rod . . .!'

Her husky groan of longing made his breath catch in his throat. 'I wish I had all night with you, Keilly,' he moaned his own desire. 'But they're waiting for us,' he added regretfully, 'and much as I want to be with you I don't want to upset your family. Will you wait here while I go and dress?'

She nodded wordlessly, feeling shattered by the emotions that had taken her so much by surprise. She hadn't chosen to love him, hadn't wanted to love him, and yet it was fact, there was nothing she could do to change it. It made her feel vulnerable and more than a little scared to know this man's welfare meant more to her than anyone else's, that she had rushed over here tonight like a love-sick fool, that she would do it again if the need should ever arise. Was this how her mother had felt about her father? If it had been perhaps she could understand a little better now.

'Ready?'

She turned with a start, not noticing the passing of time as she waited for him, loving the smooth fit of the navy blue suit he wore, his eyes darker in colour as he looked at her. She loved this man, and yet there could be no future for them, only now, before he went back to the life that took him into the public limelight he loved, a limelight she knew she could never share, not as his girlfriend or anything else he cared to make of her.

'Keilly?' he seemed puzzled by the almost lost look in her eyes.

She forced herself to act normally; Rod must never know how deeply she cared for him. 'Ready,' she agreed brightly. 'I was just wondering if it wasn't going to rain again,' she looked up pointedly at the darkening sky as they went outside.

His arm went companionably about her shoulders as they began the walk back to the car. 'Not before we get into the dry, I hope,' he said ruefully.

They took her uncle's car back to the hotel, the Jaguar still firmly stuck in the mud. She made no demur when Rod took the car keys out of her hand and drove them back, content to sit at his side.

'You aren't worried, are you?' Rod gave her a concerned glance. 'I'm sure your aunt isn't going to be too annoyed by our delay,' he grasped her hand in his. 'I did explain to her on the telephone what had happened.'

She turned to him with a start. 'I'm sure Aunt Sylvie won't be in the least annoyed. She's used to coping.'

'Then what is it?'

She swallowed hard at his perception. 'Sorry?'

He frowned. 'You seem different somehow.'

'Can't you tell when you've kissed a woman senseless?' she derided, her mouth twisted mockingly, knowing she had to pull herself together or give herself away as yet another woman who had fallen in love with him.

'That's better,' he grinned. 'I'm not used to seeing you without the light of challenge in your eyes.'

'Don't worry,' she said dryly. 'It's still there.'

They all went straight into dinner once Keilly and Rod reached the hotel, Rod nodding acknowledgement of Kathy, although it wasn't possible to converse with the other couple as they were seated at the opposite end of the table.

As her aunt had predicted everyone treated Rod just like any other guest, and as the meal progressed Keilly found herself relaxing into the role of his girlfriend, the casually intimate touches of her hand and the warm smiles he gave her being designed to show everyone that was how he thought of her.

'Pity about your car,' one of her uncle's oldest friends remarked when they were once again in the lounge, enjoying coffee and brandy this time.

Rod nodded, his arm about Keilly's waist as he held her to his side. 'I'll call a garage in the morning and get them to tow me out.'

'You mustn't go to that trouble,' Peter joined them, a reluctant Kathy at his side. 'I'm Peter Carmichael,' he held out his hand in friendly greeting. 'You're renting one of my cottages,' he explained, not seeming to notice his wife's start of surprise; Kathy obviously hadn't known until that moment that Rod was staying on the estate! 'I'll send someone over tomorrow morning with a tractor and we'll soon have your car out.'

Keilly studied the two men, Peter who had had every social advantage, private schooling, university, and Rod, who had been brought up in a middle-class family, working hard for every bit of fame and recognition he had. It was a startling contrast, and yet she could see the two men instantly liked each other.

'Thanks very much,' Rod smiled his gratitude. 'That's very kind of you.'

'Not at all,' Peter dismissed. 'I should have had that track tarmaced last summer when I had the opportunity. We don't usually get winter visitors, you see, and I'd completely forgotten the way that track goes in the winter. Oh I'm sorry, darling,' he brought Kathy forward smilingly. 'This is my wife Kathy,' he said proudly.

Rod nodded. 'We've met.'

Kathy swallowed hard, seeming to become even paler

than she already was. 'I—We have?' she choked, her eyes wide.

'At the bazaar,' he reminded smoothly, his eyes narrowing thoughtfully.

'Oh—oh yes,' she nodded, moistening her dry lips. 'I'll just go and see if I can make myself useful in the kitchen,' she excused herself, making a hasty exit before anyone could even think of stopping her.

Keilly watched her cousin as she disappeared into the kitchen, recognising all the signs of severe strain. Kathy was getting nearer and nearer to breaking, and if she did that there was no telling what she might say or do. It was an evening that was destined to be thwart with tension.

'... will nine o'clock be too early for you?' she heard the tailend of Peter's conversation, he obviously seeing nothing wrong in his wife wanting to help her mother out in the kitchen.

'Nine o'clock will be fine,' Rod nodded. 'Are you sure it won't be an inconvenience for you on a Sunday?'

Peter gave a rueful smile. 'I have a working estate, and unfortunately the animals and crops don't realise we're supposed to rest on a Sunday,' he mocked himself.

Rod laughed softly. 'I suppose not, I never thought of it that way before. It must be hard on your children if you work every day?'

'We only have the one, a daughter,' Peter's smile became indulgent. 'And Heather enjoys nothing more than coming round the estate with me. At six I suppose it's a novelty, when she's older there will probably be complaints!'

The two men were talking together as if they had known each other for years, and it wasn't something that should be encouraged. But Keilly had no idea how to prevent it. Kathy should have stayed here and helped her instead of running off like that!

'... so I wondered if you would still be here at Easter?'

Once again she came in on the tailend of Peter's conversation, although she had an idea what he was going to say next!

'I can see no reason why I shouldn't be,' Rod answered huskily. 'And a few very good ones why I should,' he was looking directly at Keilly as he said the last.

'In that case——'

'Peter, I don't think this is the time,' she interrupted sharply. 'Besides, Mr Bartlett is here on holiday.'

He frowned at her unwarranted vehemence. 'But it would only be for a few hours,' he said in a puzzled voice. 'And it would mean such a lot to how well we did.'

'Have you talked to Kathy about it?' she asked desperately. 'After all, she usually organises it, and——'

'You know I mentioned it to her the other day,' he looked even more puzzled.

'Maybe if you told me what all this is about . . .' Rod looked at them both pointedly.

'How rude of us,' Peter gave him an apologetic smile. 'You see, every Easter we hold a Fête in the garden at The Hall,' he explained. 'We usually get one of the local dignitaries to come along and open it. I realise it isn't your usual type of thing, but I've been wondering——'

'I'd love to come and open it,' Rod nodded.

Keilly looked at him with wide eyes. 'You would?'

'Why not?' he raised dark brows.

'Because—well, because——'

'Keilly and my wife thought it an awful cheek to ask you,' Peter told him. 'But I've always maintained that you never get anywhere by not asking.'

'So have I.' Rod's eyes were mocking as he looked down at Keilly.

She blushed at his double meaning. 'We just thought that as you were here on holiday,' she defended awkwardly, 'that you wouldn't want to become involved.'

'How thoughtful of you, darling,' his arm tightened about her waist as she stiffened at the endearment. 'But I don't mind in the least. In fact, I might enjoy it.'

'I hope so,' Peter said with enthusiasm. 'So we can safely put your name on our advertising sheets, can we?'

'Certainly,' Rod agreed. 'I'll look forward to it.'

'I can't tell you how pleased I am,' the other man beamed. 'I'll just go and find Kathy to tell her the good news. She's going to be thrilled!' he predicted.

Kathy was going to be far from that, and her candid reaction to her husband's news could give away more than she wanted it to! 'Why don't you two men continue talking,' it was the last thing she wanted them to do without her there to monitor their conversation, but in the circumstances it was the lesser of two evils. 'And I'll go and get Kathy,' she suggested.

'Don't be too long,' Rod said warmly as he reluctantly released her. 'I know what you women are when you get together,' he teased.

'Especially those three,' Peter joined in the teasing. 'When Sylvie and Kathy get together it's bad enough, but with Keilly as well——! We probably won't see them again for hours.'

Keilly left them to their teasing, her thoughts preoccupied. She had known, as had Kathy, that tonight was going to be awkward enough, but she was sure neither of them had envisaged Rod and Peter actually *liking* each other!

Kathy was still in the kitchen with her mother,

although it appeared they had now completed what little tidying up there had to be done.

'You go on, Mum,' Kathy encouraged as she saw Keilly's worried frown. 'We'll be out in a minute.'

'Don't be long,' she warned as she left.

'Has he gone?' Kathy hissed as soon as they were alone.

'No,' Keilly sighed. 'You know I have to drive him. He and Peter are still talking——'

'And you left them alone!' her cousin gasped. 'Are you mad? They could be comparing notes by now!'

'Kathy——'

'Come on,' she pulled Keilly along with her. 'We can't leave the two of them alone any longer. And I must say, I think you could have warned me he was staying at one of *our* cottages——'

'Kathy, will you just listen——'

'I don't have the time,' she snapped. 'I have to—Ah, darling,' she gave Peter a wan smile as they reached the two men. 'I've been looking for you.'

'I haven't moved,' he frowned.

'I have a headache, Peter,' she added tautly. 'Much as I hate to break up the party I think we should go now.'

He was instantly concerned. 'Is it very bad, darling?'

'Well of course it's bad,' she answered waspishly. 'I would hardly want to leave if it weren't.'

'No, of course not,' Peter flushed at the rebuke. 'Rod and I were just discussing the Fête at Easter——'

'I'm sure Mr Bartlett isn't interested in our little provincial affairs,' Kathy's voice was brittle.

'On the contrary, Mrs Carmichael,' he drawled. 'Your husband has asked me to open it for you.'

Keilly watched as all the colour ebbed from her cousin's face, although she could feel little real sympathy for her. If she had taken two minutes to listen she would have been forewarned. Well, it was too late now.

'Really?' Kathy's voice was harsh.

'I was only too happy to accept,' Rod nodded, his eyes narrowed. 'I imagine you would rather discuss the details some other time?'

She gave him a startled look. 'I would?'

'Your headache,' he reminded dryly.

Kathy blushed. 'Of course.' She put her hand through the crook of Peter's arm. 'I'll contact you at a later date, Mr Bartlett.'

'Any time,' he agreed. 'You know where I am.'

'Yes,' she bit out tautly. 'Peter, could we go now?'

Her husband nodded immediately. 'We'll just go and make our excuses. I'll see you in the morning, Rod,' he told the other man ruefully. 'Keilly,' he kissed her lightly on the cheek, Kathy following suit before they crossed the room to speak to her mother and father.

Rod watched them with a thoughtful expression. 'Nice couple,' he murmured.

'Yes.'

He looked down at Keilly, his expression relaxing a little. 'Good friends of yours?' he asked with casual interest.

'Very,' she was as abrupt as Kathy had been minutes earlier, not wanting to talk about the other couple.

'Does Mrs Carmichael often suffer from these headaches?'

Keilly gave him a sharp look. 'Sometimes.'

'Pity,' he drawled.

She felt a lot easier once Kathy and Peter had actually left, relaxing even more as Rod chatted easily to the other guests, completely in control of himself and the conversation. As she watched him she knew she couldn't help but fall in love with such a man. He was handsome, charming, gave her his undivided attention every time he spoke or looked at her, what woman could resist such a man? He had never shown her any of the cruelty he had Kathy and Veronica, and even when she put him down he still came back for more of the same. She couldn't help but love him!

'Is there anything the matter?' He had turned and caught her fascinated gaze on him.

'Oh—er—no,' she flushed uncomfortably. 'No, nothing. Would you like me to drive you home now?'

'Your aunt won't mind if we leave?'

'No, of course not.'

'Then I'd love you to drive me home,' he said throatily. 'Can you stay for a while?'

'Just long enough to make sure you're home,' she taunted.

'Shame,' he grimaced. 'Although probably sensible,' he added softly as they made their way over to where her aunt and uncle were deep in conversation with several other people.

'Sensible?' she queried his choice of word, arching dark brows.

'If you came into the cottage I might not want to let you out again,' he smiled.

Keilly felt her breath catch in her throat at the intimacy of that smile. 'It wouldn't be your choice,' she snapped.

He met her gaze steadily. 'Wouldn't it?'

'No!' her eyes flashed deeply grey, realising she had perhaps revealed too much of her feelings tonight, unable to hide the newness of her discovered love completely.

'Let's not argue about it,' he squeezed her waist encouragingly. 'I don't want to argue with you at all.'

All too quickly—for Keilly!—they had made their

excuses and Rod was driving them back to the cottage. She was terrified of being alone with him again, uncertain of her own reaction to him now, despite what she had told him to the contrary.

'Would you come out with me tomorrow evening?' he suddenly asked her. 'Oh not to a restaurant,' he added hastily at her withdrawn expression. 'I've learnt my lesson about that,' he said ruefully. 'No, this time I intend taking you where no one will recognise me.'

'Is there such a place?' she derided.

He smiled. 'There are many places like that,' he assured her softly. 'I'm afraid that you attracted as much attention as I in the restaurant the other evening.'

She gave him a sharp look, not able to see much in the darkness of the car. 'What do you mean?'

'You're a local girl,' he explained gently. 'People are interested to see who you're dating.'

'Is that all you meant?' she asked suspiciously.

'Of course. What else could I have meant?' he shrugged.

'Nothing,' she dismissed abruptly. 'And if you're sure we won't be stared at tomorrow night I would like to go out with you.'

'Good.'

She ignored the satisfaction in his voice. 'Maybe you could call me if Peter doesn't manage to get your car out of the mud; I could pick you up again.'

'He seems pretty confident.'

'He's a very confident man,' she agreed, suddenly wishing she hadn't brought his attention back to Kathy and Peter. But she needn't have worried, Rod had more urgent matters on his mind!

'Keilly!' He turned to her after stopping the car at the end of the driveway, switching off the engine. 'Dear God, Keilly, I've been waiting for this all evening!' He pulled her across the seat into his arms, claiming her mouth possessively.

She knew even as his tongue probed between her lips that she had too, that the hours since they had last touched like this hadn't dulled their desire for each other, their emotions flaming all too quickly out of control.

'I love you, Keilly. I love you,' Rod murmured the words over and over again against her lips before once more claiming them with a savagery that left her weak.

His declaration of love coming so quickly on top of her own realised feelings had her clinging to him as she returned his kisses with a fervour of her own, offering no resistance as he smoothed the coat from her shoulders, releasing the three buttons that were at the collar of her gown, pushing the material aside to caress the creamy curve of her breasts, finding one hardened peak beneath the lace of her bra, caressing the nipple with shuddering pleasure.

'Why don't we go into the cottage?' she suggested raggedly.

'No,' he groaned, his mouth returning to hers.

She didn't understand the reason for his rejection, and as his lips moved warmly over the throbbing peak of her breast she didn't particularly care, arching up into him, gasping slightly as his teeth bit into the sensitive flesh.

'Touch me, Keilly,' he encouraged throatily. 'Touch me the way I'm touching you!'

She needed no second bidding, quickly unbuttoning his shirt to kiss the hard flesh beneath, feeling him tremble beneath her caresses. A heady sense of power urged her to even more intimacy, and one hand moved down to the hardness of his thigh, feeling him tense beneath her touch as she began to slowly caress the throbbing evidence of his desire.

'Not here, darling,' he groaned as another shudder of ecstasy wracked his body. 'Keilly, please. I want you so badly!' He quickly removed her hand, a fine sheen of perspiration to his brow as he fought for control of rapidly spiralling emotions.

'I want you too,' she choked her disappointment.

'But this isn't the bed I once promised you, is it?' he gently chided.

'The cottage——'

'I want you to be sure,' his fingertips over her lips prevented further speech. 'I want you to be very sure before we make love, because once I've made you mine I never intend to let you go again.'

She blinked up at him in the darkness, sanity returning quickly now that he was no longer kissing her. 'What—what do you mean?' she asked shakily.

'Whatever I do, wherever I go in future, I want you to be with me,' he told her gently, smoothing back the hair at her temples. 'But you have to want it too.'

'But I——'

'It's still too soon for you, I know that,' he silenced her once again. 'But it will work out, you'll see.' He rebuttoned her dress for her with hands that weren't quite steady. 'Just trust me, Keilly. Trust me,' he kissed her lingeringly on the lips before getting out of the car, except for the dark glow of his eyes looking none the worse for their passionate encounter. 'I'll see you tomorrow, darling,' he bent forward to say. 'About seven. And have your dinner first,' he advised.

'But——'

'I love you, Keilly.'

She drew in a ragged breath, only just managing to hold back her own declaration. If he ever knew she loved him in return he would never let her go until he had made her his completely. 'Tomorrow,' she agreed abruptly.

She sat and watched until the lights were all switched on inside the cottage, telling herself she was just making sure he got in all right, all the time knowing her delay was because she was shaking too much to drive anywhere just yet!

CHAPTER SEVEN

As they approached the brightly lit cinema, with its advertising posters outside announcing the showing of 'Beginning Again' starring Rod Bartlett and Cindy Peters, Keilly knew there could be no doubt that this was where Rod was taking her.

About his declaration of love she had tried not to think during the long night and day that had passed since she had last seen him. Such a declaration could mean anything or nothing, and she didn't know Rod well enough to know which it was. Even if it was the former it didn't change anything between them, they still had as much separating them as before. But now they had more than she could cope with drawing them together!

Going to see him naked in a film wasn't something she wanted right now, not when she already felt so vulnerable! The coloured posters called it a love story, showing Rod and Cindy naked from the waist up, their arms around each other as they looked deeply into each other's eyes. It was blatantly provocative, and Keilly could feel herself blushing as she sensed Rod looking at her.

She shook her head. 'I don't think——'

'Give it a chance, Keilly,' he encouraged softly. 'I admit this poster makes it look other than it is, but that's just the advertising department encouraging cinema-goers.'

'You mean your name isn't enough?'

'Now, now,' he chided at her sarcasm. 'Don't get

bitchy. Give the film a chance, Keilly. I can almost guarantee you'll love it.'

'It's the *almost* I'm worried about,' she said dryly. 'And I thought you said you were taking me somewhere where you would be inconspicuous?' she reminded.

Rod grinned, looking pointedly at the other people crowding into the cinema, none of them taking the slightest bit of notice of them as they talked together. 'Who would expect me to be going to see my own film?' he derided.

'True,' she drawled.

He gave a rueful smile. 'It's the only way I'll ever get you to see it.'

'I haven't gone in yet,' she reminded him, glancing at the posters once again. The sight of him making love to another woman wasn't a pleasant one.

Some of her emotions must have shown in her face, Rod tilting her face up towards his with his hand under her chin. 'It's only acting, Keilly,' he told her softly. 'Cindy is very much involved with someone else.'

'And you?'

His eyes darkened to navy blue. 'I'm in love with you.'

He sounded so sure of his feelings, so *certain*! 'I meant then,' she said tightly.

'Keilly, no one can feel in the least romantic when your every move is being watched by a dozen or so other people,' he sighed. 'Cindy and I were working, that's all it was to us. I wish you would trust me, darling,' he added gently. 'Trust me enough to come and see the film with me. If you hate it I promise we can leave, any time you want to.'

When he put it like that it was churlish to refuse, and within a few minutes they had paid their money, bought their sweets and drinks, and taken their seats in the relative darkness of the cinema just as the film was about to begin.

'Just in time,' Rod murmured, lacing her fingers through his as he held her hand firmly in his.

Keilly was determined not to like the film, was sure she wasn't going to, and yet almost from the first moment she was riveted to the screen, to the struggles of a woman starting her life again when her husband and two children were killed in a car crash. At thirty-five she suddenly found herself alone for the first time in fifteen years, afraid to face the future, too hurt to live in the past with her memories. Her life had changed dramatically in a matter of a few minutes, the town she had been brought up in and lived in all her life her only reality. Then a man called Ben Kingsfield came to the town, with radical plans for construction, intent on changing the little she had left.

The situation was further complicated for Sara by Ben's obvious attraction to her, not understanding her need to keep the town as it was. There had been nothing she could do to stop him, and even as she tried she knew he was a man who would win, in everything he set out to do. But, as Ben made his intention to make her live again clear, Sara became afraid of something else, afraid most of all of replacing her husband with another man, full of the insecurities of having loved and been loved by one man, whereas Ben could have his pick of woman, and often had.

It was a poignant and moving story, and Keilly was soon so engrossed in it that she forgot her surroundings, forgot even the man at her side, tears cascading down her cheeks as Sara gave herself into Ben's care, as she entrusted all her present and future happiness into his hands. And Ben hadn't let her down, making love to her tenderly, beautifully, promising her that no matter where they might be they would be together from now on, that just as the world moved on so did life, that Sara was truly 'beginning again'.

Keilly felt sure there wasn't a dry eye in the cinema as the film came to an end, the tissue in her hand soaked to a soggy lump, her emotions frayed.

She followed Rod from the cinema, his hand firm on her arm as he guided her through the crowd. They hadn't spoken at all during the showing of the film, and they didn't speak now, Rod respecting her need for a few minutes to collect her thoughts together after being so emotionally moved.

'I owe you an apology,' she said in the stillness of his car, Rod making no effort to go out of the car park yet, everyone else seeming to have that idea, making a tailback of traffic. She turned to look at him in the shadowed darkness. 'I was completely wrong about the film.'

'And the nude scene?' he prompted softly.

She blinked her confusion. 'I—er—It was so much a part of the story, so necessary, that I didn't even realise . . .' She shook her head. 'I didn't realise,' she repeated dazedly, knowing it was true. It had been important for Ben to make love to Sara, to give her the confidence in herself and their love, that it had seemed a natural continuation of events, and had been nothing like the crudity Keilly had assumed it would be before she had seen the film. 'I owe you an apology for that too,' she said huskily. 'It was a beautiful film, all of it.'

'Thank you,' was all Rod said with quiet sincerity.

She gave him a sharp look. 'No "I told you so's"? No gloating that I was so wrong?'

He shook his head. 'It's enough that you liked it. But even if you hadn't it would have made no difference, you're entitled to your opinion, as you once reminded me,' he added dryly, starting the engine as the queue to leave the car park was down to three cars.

Keilly looked down at her hands. 'I think you deserve to win the Oscar.'

He turned to give her a grateful smile as he manoeuvred the Jaguar out into the high street. 'It's nice of you to say so.'

She turned in her seat. 'I mean it,' she said with unwarranted fervour.

'I know you do,' he said quietly.

'Rod——'

'Yes?' he frowned at her hesitation.

She swallowed hard. 'Will you tell me—tell me about Veronica?' She watched him anxiously, not sure how he would react to such a request.

His frown deepened. 'Are you sure you really want to know?'

'Yes. Could we go back to the cottage now?'

He drew in a ragged breath. 'I'm not sure that's a good idea in the circumstances.'

'Please!' she put her hand on his thigh, instantly feeling him tense beneath her. 'Please,' she repeated as he turned to look at her.

He nodded wordlessly, his expression grim as they made the two mile journey to the cottage. But Keilly couldn't refute wanting to know about Veronica, needing to know about at least that part of his past. And he would be the first person to admit that his relationship with Veronica King had helped shape him into the man he was today.

'Go through to the lounge,' he invited abruptly once they reached the cottage. 'I'll make us some coffee; I think we're going to need it.'

She didn't offer to help him, realising he needed the time alone, that talking about Veronica was going to be as difficult for him as it was for her. No matter what else she knew about Rod she was sure he was a highly sensitive man, that he felt deeply about things and people. It was becoming more and more difficult for her to associate him with the man Kathy described. The two men sounded alien to each other.

They faced each other across the lounge like adversaries, Rod putting a match to the fire, the leaping flames adding a cheery warmth to the room. Keilly poured the coffee, and for a few minutes they eyed each other warily above the rims of their cups, both loath to speak.

Finally Rod was the one to sigh. 'I didn't realise how difficult this was going to be.'

'If you would rather not——'

'No!' his voice was sharp. 'No,' he spoke more calmly now, searching for the right words to begin. 'Do you trust me, Keilly? Do you finally trust me?'

She swallowed hard, determined to answer truthfully. 'I'm trying to. I really am trying.'

His dark gaze searched her pale face. 'It's enough,' he nodded. 'It has to be,' he sighed. 'I was almost twenty-one when I met Veronica, as you know she was already over thirty. A friend of mine knew of a party where a famous producer was going to be,' he shrugged. 'So we gatecrashed. I gatecrashed a lot of parties in those days,' he recalled ruefully. 'I was a nobody, I certainly wasn't going to get a legitimate invite! This particular party was a little different from most, every guest a "name" of some repute; Dave and I were sure to be found out for what we were,' he grimaced. 'We had been there about half an hour when two big muscle-bound men came over and "politely" asked us to leave. Dave was about to argue when Veronica stepped in and said we were her guests for the evening.'

Keilly's eyes widened. 'And what was how you first met?'

'Yes,' he smiled at the memory. 'She told me afterwards that she had been trying to find out who I was with ever since she had arrived ten minutes earlier,' he chuckled softly. 'Veronica was a very forthright lady, if she wanted something she said so.'

'She wanted you,' Keilly guessed flatly.

He gave her a narrow-eyed look. 'Yes, she wanted me. And I wanted her. Did you ever see any of her pictures?'

'She was beautiful,' Keilly nodded.

'Inside as well as out,' he stated firmly. 'She grew up in Hollywood society, both her parents were "stars" in their day, and Veronica was in front of the cameras before she even learnt to talk. She had been through it all in her thirty years, the drugs scene, the permissiveness, a miscarriage, a marriage break-down, and yet she had somehow still managed to stay beautiful. I never heard her say anything bitchy about anyone in the three years we were together. But she wasn't a paragon either,' his thoughts were inwards, his eyes glowing with memories. 'She could be fun. She loved nothing better than playing practical jokes on people. That was how she taught me to laugh at myself, not to take life too seriously. The three years I knew her were the best in my life.'

'Did she—did she love you too?'

'Yes,' he answered flatly. 'Yes, she loved me.'

'Tell me why she—why she died?'

Deep lines became grooved beside his mouth and nose. 'I asked her to marry me; we were in love, it seemed the natural thing to do. She turned me down flat, gave me every excuse but the real one. Eighteen months after we had begun living together she had found out she had cancer,' he revealed grimly.

'Oh no,' Keilly gasped her horror.

'Yes,' he confirmed harshly. 'There was nothing they could do, they gave her a year at most. She didn't tell me, and for the next eighteen months I continued to live in a fool's paradise, thought we had our whole lives together. The day before she—before the accident she told me the truth. I knew there was something wrong with her, she was beginning to tire easily, to lose weight; but the real reason for it never occurred to me! She was so young and beautiful, it didn't seem possible she was dying. I wanted to take her to every specialist there was, I was willing to try anything to keep her alive.'

'But Veronica wasn't,' Keilly prompted softly, seeing how deeply he was being affected by what he was telling her.

He shook his head. 'She knew there was nothing that could be done. Although she told me she would try them all if that was what I wanted. The next day she took her plane up and never came back; it crashed into the sea. She left a note telling me she couldn't put me through the pain and disillusionment going to those specialists would entail. Put *me* through it!' He dropped his face down into his hands. 'I would have done anything for her.'

Keilly moved across the room, sitting on the floor at his feet, her hands resting comfortingly on his legs. 'Except let her die,' she told him gently. 'Rod, she didn't want to go through all those disappointments, all those times of being told there was nothing they could do to help her, and she didn't want you to go through it either.'

He put his hands down slowly. 'You understand. You really do,' he said slowly.

'My mother died of heart disease,' she recalled flatly. 'She was young too, about Veronica's age, and they told her there was nothing they could do for her either. None of us knew until after she died how ill she had been for so long, she hid it from us all.'

Rod's eyes were darkly troubled. 'It wasn't an hereditary disease, was it?'

She frowned. 'No . . .'

'Thank God!' He shuddered, his hands moving to grasp both of hers. 'I couldn't bear it if I lost you too!'

'Oh no, darling,' she sat up to hold him against her breasts. 'I'm not going to die,' she assured him huskily. 'I'm not going anywhere.'

'You called me darling,' his voice was muffled against her. 'Did you mean it?' He moved back to look at her, searching the beautiful vulnerability of her face.

'Yes,' she told him evenly. 'I meant it.'

'I love you,' he groaned as his head bent to hers.

Emotions were running very high, quickly spiralling out of control as their kisses became savagely heated, demanding more and more of each other, becoming impatient with the hindrance of their clothing as they sought closer contact.

'I meant what I said a few minutes ago,' she told him raggedly. 'I'm not going anywhere, and especially not now.'

Blue eyes clashed with grey as he searched her face for the meaning of her words. 'Are you sure?' he finally asked breathlessly.

'Rod,' she chided teasingly. 'Do I have to beg to be seduced?'

His expression remained serious. 'You have to be very sure. If you stay now you'll remain mine.'

'I'm not making this decision lightly——'

'I know that,' he soothed.

'No, you don't,' she shook her head, as sober as he now. 'I never knew my father, in fact I don't even know who he was. My mother never liked to talk about him, and she died before I was really old enough to ask questions. But growing up illegitimate has made me more aware of the mistakes that can be made when people go into a physical relationship without considering all the consequences. It isn't a decision I would *ever* make lightly,' she repeated vehemently.

His hands tenderly framed her face. 'I won't ever let anything like that happen to you,' he promised.

She met his gaze trustingly. 'I know you won't.'

'You love me.'

'I——'

His fingertips over her lips prevented further speech. 'You love me, Keilly,' he stated firmly. 'Even if you don't know it yet.'

She knew it, God she knew it. And yet she couldn't actually say the words. But she didn't need to as Rod stood up to swing her into his arms before striding up the stairs with her to his bedroom.

She knew only a moment of panic as he began to undress her before the warm love in his eyes drove all other thoughts but him out of her mind, helping him with the last of her clothing before he too began to undress. She already knew the beauty of his body, had been witness to it the evening he joined her for her swim, his male beauty riveting on the cinema screen. But tonight he was hers, and hers alone, and as she began to touch him she knew he was everything she had ever wanted in the man she loved.

'You're beautiful, Keilly,' Rod caressed her wonderingly in the semi-darkness of the room. 'Beautiful—and innocent.'

The last was added as a question, and Keilly blushed her reply, burying her face against his hair-roughened chest.

'I'm glad,' he murmured into her hair. 'It's never mattered to me before, but with you it does. I'll be gentle, my darling. I promise.'

As they lay on the bed side by side she began to lose her shyness with him, caressing the hardness of his back and hips even as he began to kiss her throat and breasts. His were the only lips that had ever touched her this intimately, and she felt the now familiar warmth as his mouth closed moistly over one taut nipple, flicking his tongue against the sensitive flesh as she quivered her pleasure.

But the intimacy of his kisses had far from ended, and as he moved lower down her body she began to stiffen with alarm, squirming away from him in panic.

'Trust me.' Rod's hands on her arms attempted to still her. 'I would never do anything to hurt you. Trust me, Keilly,' he urged as he had numerous times before.

She stilled beneath the intensity of his words, her uncertainty reflected in her eyes as she felt his lips against the flatness of her stomach, tensing as he moved even lower, gasping out loud as she felt his lips where no other man had ever touched, her gasp turning to a groan of delight as pleasure such as she had never known wracked her body, making her tremble with desire.

As he moved up her body to once again kiss her lips her senses were filled with the musky scent of their heated bodies, hardly aware that he nudged her legs apart, of the hardness of his desire throbbing against her as he waited for entry into her warmth.

He was waiting for her, for that final sign that would bind her to him. Her gaze fixed steadily on his she raised herself until he possessed her, her small cry lost in his groan of pleasure, forgotten as he began to move gently, surely, within her. His movements were slow at first, increasing in tempo as her breath came in tortured gasps, capturing her mouth with his as he felt her tense, his tongue plundering the warm moistness even as she shuddered to a convulsive climax so shattering she felt weak, fresh shudders coursing through her as she felt him reach his own heady ecstasy.

They lay satiated in each other's arms, breathing deeply, still joined together, both loath to lose that contact.

'You're the most beautiful woman I've ever known,' Rod gazed down at her lovingly.

She looked up at him shyly. 'Maybe I'm a wanton, after all.'

'After making love only once?' he teased. 'I think it's too soon to tell.'

She buried her face against the dampness of his chest. 'I don't,' she said huskily.

He gave a deep groan. 'God, Keilly, I want you again!'

She knew that, her eyes widening as she felt the desire ebbing back into his body, feeling his tension within her, raising her face to his for his kiss, her lips parted invitingly.

He seemed to hesitate. 'You aren't too—uncomfortable?'

She shook her head, blushing prettily. 'No. You were so patient and loving with me that all I feel is lethargy.'

'Not for long, I hope,' he growled.

His words proved correct, their second time together slower as they took their time arousing each other, Rod showing her how to caress him in return, a lesson she was an avid pupil of, soon hearing him beg for mercy as he lay beneath her.

'You *are* a wanton!' he gasped as her legs wrapped

about his urged him deeper and deeper into her, the thrusts of his body becoming harder as she arched against him in spasmodic ecstasy, taking him along on the tide with her.

'*You're* wanton,' she corrected as they lay replete in each other's arms, smoothing his hair back from the dampness of his forehead.

He shook his head. 'My untamed sea witch.'

'Untamed?' she quirked dark brows.

'Untamed,' he nodded. 'I'll never succeed in taming you. And I don't want to. I love you just the way you are.'

She still couldn't say the words back to him, had never said them to anyone. But she thought he knew how she felt about him, was sure that he did.

'Do you have any idea what the time is?' The thought suddenly occurred to her.

He glanced at his wrist-watch. 'Just after twelve——'

'I have to go——'

'Can't you stay?' he pleaded softly, his disappointment reflected in his eyes.

'My aunt and uncle are expecting me.'

'Forget I ever asked,' he softly caressed her lips with his fingertips. 'Of course you have to go home; I'm just being greedy. I don't ever want to let you go,' he admitted ruefully. 'But for the moment I realise I have to.'

They dressed in silence, the warmth in their faces whenever they looked at each other enough for now, their communication made without words.

'Thank you for telling me about Veronica,' she told him once they reached the hotel.

He turned in his seat to look at her, his arm along the back of her seat as his hand gently caressed her nape beneath the darkness of her hair. 'Thank *you* for telling me about your father. It isn't something you like to talk about, is it?'

She blushed at his perception. 'It's made me—shy of attention.'

'Like being stared at in restaurants,' he nodded understandingly. 'I realised afterwards what was wrong; I could have kicked myself for being so insensitive!'

Keilly's eyes were wide in her pale face. 'You—already—knew—about my father?'

He nodded. 'I was born here, remember?'

Several times she tried to speak, then she just buried her face against his chest. It was too much on top of everything else that had happened tonight. What if it was knowing about her mother and father that had made him believe she would be willing to have an affair with him? She looked at him with tear-filled eyes.

'No,' he denied desperately. 'Oh no, darling,' he repeated with intense feeling. 'Don't even think it.'

'But——'

'I love *you*,' he kissed her gently. 'I want to spend my whole life with you. Whatever the circumstances of your birth it isn't important to me, in any way. I'm only sorry you've found it difficult to live with.'

'I'm not ashamed of it,' she denied quickly. 'It's just——'

'Other people can be cruel, especially when you're young,' he soothed gently. 'But can't you see that it isn't important to us?'

He was a man with supreme self-confidence, a man who cared little what others thought of him, but she didn't have his confidence, and she knew it would always matter to her.

'All that's important is that we love each other,' he added encouragingly. 'And we do, don't we?' he prompted firmly.

Keilly had difficulty swallowing, knowing that this time he wanted an answer. 'I've already told you,' once again she was evasive, 'I didn't go to bed with you lightly.'

'But——'

'I have to go in now, Rod.'

He looked displeased, although he didn't push her any further. 'I'll call you tomorrow. Maybe we can spend the day together?'

'Perhaps,' she nodded. 'I'm not sure.'

'Keilly . . .!' He stopped her as she would have got out of the car, gently caressing her cheek with sensitive fingertips. 'I'm still not rushing you, darling,' he told her huskily. 'Tonight doesn't have to be repeated unless you want it to be.'

'Rod——'

His quick kiss on the mouth silenced her. 'Sleep on it, sweetheart. Don't make any decisions—about *anything*—just now.'

Sleep was something that didn't come easily to her that night, and when it did come to her it was restless and filled with dreams, terrible dreams that still haunted her when she woke up. The sea beckoned her as never before, and she escaped from the hotel shortly after seven, too troubled to swim, simply walking miles along the deserted beach.

She arrived at The Hall shortly after nine, Kathy alone in the breakfast room, Peter already out at work on the estate, Heather at school. Keilly was glad of their absence, it was Kathy she wanted to talk to.

'Sit down, for heaven's sake,' her cousin invited impatiently as Keilly restlessly paced the room. 'What on earth is the matter with you?' she frowned as Keilly made no effort to do so. 'You look dreadful,' she realised.

She knew that, the mirror in her bedroom had told her so before she left this morning. But she cared little for her appearance, wanted only to hear the truth now. 'Kathy, did Rod really lie and cheat to get you into bed with him?'

Her cousin blanched, moving quickly to close the door. 'For goodness' sake mind what you say here,' she snapped, her brown eyes blazing. 'Anyone could have been walking by——'

'Answer me, Kathy,' she sighed her impatience. 'Did Rod really seduce you and then let you down?'

'I don't see——'

'Answer me!'

'Yes, damn it, yes!' Kathy bit out forcefully. 'I've already told you he did.'

'I know that. But——'

'You don't believe me,' her cousin realised dully. 'After all that you know I've suffered these last months you think I've been lying to you!'

'Not lying exactly,' she denied awkwardly. 'But it did happen ten years ago, it could have become confused in your mind. You could be mistaken——'

'I am not mistaken about the only other man I've ever slept with besides Peter,' Kathy said furiously. 'It isn't the sort of thing you forget,' she added bitterly.

This was the answer she had been afraid of, Rod had explained away Veronica but somehow she still couldn't reconcile herself to the way he had hurt Kathy. He had admitted that he was a different person then, a user, that he knew some of the women he slept with didn't consider their relationships in the casual light that he did, and she had hoped Kathy had been one of the latter, that it had been her cousin who had mistaken the relationship for more than it was. But Kathy was adamant it hadn't been like that, and she had to believe her.

'He really told you he loved you, that he wanted to marry you?' she had to try one last time.

'Yes!' Kathy snapped. 'How many more times do I have to tell you?'

'None,' she said dully. 'I'm sorry.'

'For what? Keilly, what's going on?' she demanded as Keilly turned to leave. 'You and he were very friendly on Saturday, you haven't been silly enough to fall for him, have you?'

'No,' she denied quickly, although she was very much afraid her face blushed her guilt for her. 'No, of course not. I just found it difficult to believe he was the type of man to use such subterfuge. He—he doesn't seem the type.'

'If a man is desperate enough he'll tell you anything!'

Those words echoed round and round in her brain as she slowly made her way back to the hotel. Had Rod lied to her to get his own way? If he had she hadn't needed much convincing, which made what had happened as much her fault as it was his. But it must never happen again. Last night had been a mistake, she knew that now. And he must be made to realise it too.

'Rod has been telephoning you every ten minutes since nine o'clock,' her aunt informed her on her return at five minutes to ten. 'That will be him again,' she predicted dryly as the phone began to ring again. 'I'll let you answer it,' she disappeared into the kitchen.

'Keilly, at last!' Rod instantly recognised her voice. 'Where have you been, darling?' he demanded to know. 'I've been worried about you.'

She moistened suddenly dry lips, her hand tightly clutching the receiver. 'I went for a walk,' she told him huskily.

'Along the beach, hmm,' he guessed lightly. 'I should have thought of that, then I could have joined you.'

'No! I mean—I wanted to be alone.'

'Keilly?' his voice sharpened with concern. 'Darling, you're all right, aren't you?'

'Of course,' she answered abruptly, her heart silently breaking into a thousand pieces. Even supposing she could ever overcome her fear of being stared at and talked about she knew she could never live with the fact that he had deceived and hurt Kathy. In the cold light of day, away from the seduction of his love, she knew that to be the truth.

'You don't sound it,' he rasped. 'I'm coming over.'

'I wish you wouldn't,' her hand shook. Would she be brave enough to tell him to his face that it was over between them? She had to be!

'I'll be there in ten minutes,' he promised grimly before ringing off.

Keilly put her own receiver down more slowly. She had to be strong about this, for the sake of everyone involved.

CHAPTER EIGHT

'THERE's really nothing to talk about,' she was telling him ten minutes later, the two of them alone in the lounge. 'Last night was a mistake, I think we should both accept it as such.'

'Like hell I will!' Rod had become more and more haggard as she spoke, his denial now a choked cry.

'Yes,' she insisted firmly. 'I'm sure you must have made mistakes in the past, well this one was mine,' she dismissed lightly. 'Put it down to the eroticism of the film I had just watched——'

'No!' his reply was more vehement this time. 'I can't believe you would ever enter into a physical relationship because you had just seen me nude in a film!'

'Because of my father?' she said abruptly.

'Yes!'

'But I'm only human, Rod, and like I said, I can make mistakes.'

His mouth was a thin angry line. 'The next thing you'll be telling me is that you made love with me because you felt sorry for me, because of what I had just told you about Veronica and myself!'

'No!' she groaned her horror of such a suggestion. 'That isn't true,' she said vehemently.

'I know that,' he nodded tautly. 'So suppose we get to the real reason for your change of mind?'

Her gaze was suddenly evasive. 'I don't know what you mean. I've just told you——'

Rod gave a deep sigh, his hands clenched into fists at his sides as he fought for control. 'You know what I mean, Keilly, and so do I, although to a lesser degree, I admit.'

She gave him a startled look, not encouraged by his grim expression. 'I have no idea what you're talking about——'

'Your cousin, Keilly,' he interrupted quietly. 'We're talking about your cousin,' he repeated firmly. 'Kathy Carmichael.'

'You—know?'

'That you're related?' he arched dark brows. 'Yes, I know,' he nodded.

Keilly's gaze was riveted to his strained face, her thoughts racing, only Rod was able to answer all the questions she had. 'How long——' she cleared her throat noisily. 'How long have you known Kathy is my cousin?'

He shrugged. 'Your aunt mentioned her daughter the first night I was here, before I came looking for you on the beach,' he added as he guessed what was going to be her next question. 'But I knew before that. You see, I thought it was Kathy I was coming here to see, I had no idea until I got here that the K. Grant in the letter to the magazine was Kathy's young cousin.'

Her palms felt damp, the dreadful reality of what he was telling her hitting her slowly. 'You thought Kathy wrote the letter?' she asked haltingly.

'Yes,' he admitted heavily. 'And if it was I wanted to know why it had been written.'

'You don't know?' Keilly accused. 'After what you did to her?'

His eyes narrowed to steely slits. 'What did I do to her?' he asked quietly.

Keilly became flushed with anger, her eyes flashing her indignation. '*Now* I can see the man she described to me! Before I found it difficult to reconcile myself to you acting so callously, now I can see just how easily you could do it. I suppose you've found it very amusing watching Kathy and I squirm as we tried to keep the truth from you, that you've enjoyed playing your little game?'

'I haven't been playing, because there is no game,' he bit out abruptly. 'I want to know why Kathy felt it necessary to pretend we have never met before?'

'You expect her to be proud of it?'

'Keilly, will you just tell me what I'm supposed to have done to Kathy?' he demanded impatiently. 'I knew her several years ago, yes, but——'

'"Knew" being the operative word,' she bit out.

'I see,' he expelled a slow breath. 'Surely you aren't going to hold that against me? Kathy and I were both young, we were different people then.'

'She may have been, but you weren't!'

'Keilly, I've already told you I can't change the past, that I've done things I'm not proud of. Although making love to Kathy was not one of them. The only thing I wish I could change about that is the fact that she's your cousin.'

'And she wishes she had never met you!' Keilly told him vehemently, her eyes stormy grey.

'That's been obvious,' he said dryly. 'I just wish someone would tell me why.'

'Don't pretend with me——'

'I am not pretending,' he told her fiercely, his fingers digging into her arms as he shook her slightly. 'Tell me what I'm supposed to have done to her!'

'The same as you did with countless other women, I should think,' she said with distaste. 'You told her you loved her, implied you were serious about her, went to bed with her, and then didn't see her again!'

Rod released her slowly, staring at her as if he had

never seen her before. He frowned darkly, turning away from her, his hands now thrust into the hip pockets of his close-fitting denims, his dark blue shirt stretched tautly across his chest and shoulders.

'I see you don't attempt to deny it,' she scorned bitterly. 'I think that's as well when you so obviously moved in with Veronica King only weeks after seducing Kathy.'

'Yes, I did, didn't I,' he agreed softly.

He was too calm, much too controlled. His fierceness or his anger she could cope with, this calmness she didn't like at all!

He turned suddenly, his eyes narrowed to steely slits. 'So *that's* what she told you,' he grated. 'At first,' he sighed. 'I imagined all sorts of things, especially when you made such scathing remarks about men like me caring only for their own selfish needs, how they left the woman afterwards not caring if she were pregnant or not.'

'Well it's the truth,' she snapped.

'I made sure Kathy wouldn't become pregnant.'

'But she said——'

'I don't give a damn what Kathy said or didn't say,' he dismissed coldly. 'Just as I think you should realise that your own reaction to this is so strong because you yourself didn't have a father. I knew I couldn't have fathered any child of Kathy's, although for a while you did have me worried. Heather being only six years old put an end to that idea.' He shrugged. 'Maybe Kathy really did think I had put her at risk, she was very innocent——'

'So innocent she believed you when you said you loved her!'

His eyes were glacial. 'Not that innocent,' he said abruptly.

Kathy blushed. 'You seduced her with your lies.'

'As I seduced you?' he prompted hardly, his jaw clenched as he waited for her answer.

'No,' she admitted quietly. 'I knew exactly what I was doing——'

'So did I,' he interrupted grimly. 'Which is why I think you should believe me about Kathy. If I can remember to take precautions with you, the woman I love, you can be sure I would be rational enough to use them with other women.'

'You thought you loved Kathy at the time——'

'Never,' he denied implacably. 'She was attractive and we liked each other, that was all there was to it. If I had realised she was a virgin you can be sure I would never have touched her,' he rasped.

'Don't tell me you actually had some guilt feelings about her,' Keilly scorned.

'No.'

'I thought not,' she derided contemptuously.

'She knew what she was doing.' He shook his head. 'You don't know the full story, Keilly, you only know what your cousin has chosen to tell you.'

'There's more?' she rasped.

'Much more,' he nodded. 'But it isn't my place to tell it to you.'

'Isn't it a little late to play the gentleman where Kathy is concerned?'

Anger flared briefly in the blue depths of his eyes, although it was quickly under control. 'Your cousin has really poisoned your mind against me. Have you ever stopped to consider she may not be telling you the complete truth?'

'Kathy is my cousin——'

'And I'm your lover,' he reminded fiercely. 'Doesn't that mean anything to you?'

Of course it meant something to her, she had known before they made love all that she was accusing him of now, but for a few hours it had ceased to matter. But it mattered now, and there could be no future for them together.

'Keilly, answer me!' He shook her as she didn't—or couldn't—answer him. 'What do I mean to you?'

She moistened her lips, swallowing hard. 'You were my lover——'

'Are,' he corrected determinedly. 'I told you there would be no going back once I had made you mine. You belong to me now.'

'Did you tell Kathy that too?' she scorned.

For a moment he looked as if she had hit him, pushing her away from him so suddenly she almost fell, regaining her balance with effort. 'Your cousin didn't tell you the true version of what happened between us ten years ago,' he rasped.

'Then you tell it to me now,' she invited again.

'I can't do that,' he shook his head. 'I think you should talk to Kathy about it.'

'I've already talked to her about it,' Keilly insisted stubbornly.

'You aren't even willing to give me enough of the benefit of the doubt to ask her about it again?' His eyes were compelling, forcing her to answer him.

'No,' she said flatly.

He drew in a deep shuddering breath. 'Then that's that, isn't it?'

'Yes.'

He shrugged, very pale beneath his tan. 'If you ever feel like asking Kathy for the truth you can reach me afterwards in London,' he gave her the telephone number. 'If I'm not there leave a message on my answering machine and I'll call you back.'

Keilly gave him a startled look. 'You aren't leaving Selchurch?'

His gaze was steady. 'It seems I have no further reason to stay.'

'But I—You're going now?' she was astounded.

'Yes.'

'But——'

'Don't worry,' he derided at her worried expression. 'I'll be back in time for the Fête. It was a promise, after all.'

'But you don't have to leave just because—just because——'

'Just because even though we're lovers, even though you know I love you, you choose to believe someone else's word over mine?' he finished harshly.

'Kathy is my cousin!' she repeated desperately, little dreaming he would be walking out of her life so quickly.

'You already know the answer to that,' he said wearily. 'Goodbye, Keilly. Don't forget to call me if you change your mind.'

She was still sitting in the armchair she had dropped down into after his departure when her aunt came into the room.

'Has Rod left?' she realised with regret. 'I was just going to offer him some coffee.'

'He had to go,' somehow Keilly managed to find her voice, although it wasn't easy. Rod had implied that Kathy was the one lying about the past, but the other woman was her cousin, had been her best friend for the past fifteen years, she couldn't have lied to her about something so important! 'He's gone back to London for several weeks,' she added hardly.

'Again?' her aunt frowned. 'He works much too hard.'

'He didn't say anything about working.'

Her aunt gave a worried glance at Keilly's pale face. 'The two of you haven't argued, have you?' she probed gently. 'Only I couldn't help noticing how friendly the two of you have become since he came back this time.'

'We were just friends,' Keilly dismissed abruptly. 'You must know that I could never become involved with someone so much in the public limelight as Rod,' she added with a resolve she was far from feeling.

Her aunt frowned again. 'Isn't it time you put those old prejudices behind you?'

'*I* have, it's other people who still find my background so interesting.'

'Are you sure?' Aunt Sylvie said gently. 'What happened to your mother happens to thousands of women every year now, and they are thought none the worse for it.'

'What *did* happen to my mother?' she looked pleadingly at her aunt. 'Did she love my father or was it just a chance meeting that mistakenly resulted in me?'

Her aunt's expression softened. 'This is the first time you've shown such interest in the past.'

'It's the first time it's been so important to me!'

Her aunt sat down in the chair opposite her. 'Your mother always told me that once you were really old enough to understand, and if you really wanted to know, that you should be told the truth. Before I've always sensed in you a resentment, a distinct lack of understanding for your mother's feelings. That isn't there now,' she smiled. 'I think you've finally grown up, Keilly.'

She knew she had, the resentment she had always felt towards her mother now replaced with the knowledge of what it was like to love a man so much you *ached* to belong to him. She had loved in the same way, she felt she could now understand her mother. 'Is my father still alive?'

'Probably,' Aunt Sylvie nodded. 'But he never knew of your existence, Keilly, so if you plan to go looking for him I would recommend caution,' she warned.

'There's no point in looking for a father I've never known, we would be strangers to each other,' she shook her head. 'But tell me about them. Did they love each other?'

'I think so, yes. Your mother certainly loved your father. He was up here working for his company, missing his wife and son dreadfully——'

'He was *married*?' Keilly gasped.

'Separated,' her aunt corrected. 'His wife had left him several months previous to his coming here. He was lonely, your mother fell in love with him, and he seemed very fond of her too.'

'You knew him?'

'He was staying here when they met.' Her aunt sighed. 'His wife changed her mind, decided she wanted to resume the marriage, and because of their little boy he thought they should too. By this time your mother already knew she was pregnant, but she decided not to tell him, that it would be better for everyone if she didn't. I think she was right. To have told your father the truth would have pulled him apart, and in the end no one would have been happy.'

'I—If——' she moistened her lips. 'If my mother had told him about me do you think he would have stayed with her?'

'I think so,' Aunt Sylvie nodded. 'Estelle knew it too, which was why she didn't tell him. In the end he could only have resented her for making him choose between his son and his daughter.'

Keilly nodded, feeling very close to her mother in

that moment. 'I would have done the same thing she did.'

'I know,' her aunt smiled. 'I hope you can see now that you have nothing to be ashamed of?'

'I don't think I was ever actually ashamed,' she replied slowly. 'I just didn't understand.'

Her aunt stood up. 'Until this moment you didn't want to. Oh you always loved your mother, but you resented her too for making you different to other children. Your feelings for Rod have matured you, in more ways than one. If they hadn't I would never have told you about your mother.'

'Why not?' she frowned.

'Because Estelle deserved your understanding, not your contempt.' She shrugged. 'Until today you could only give her the latter.'

She knew it was the truth, but having loved Rod in the same way her mother had loved her father she could understand what had made her mother make the decisions she had. In the circumstances she would have made exactly the same decisions herself.

Time dragged slowly after Rod's departure, although Kathy finally seemed to be relaxing a little in his absence. Keilly had mixed feelings about his return in April, knew that she wanted to see him again, but feared it too. He despised her now, could do no other.

'You aren't looking at all well lately,' Kathy frowned at her one afternoon about six weeks after Rod's departure.

Keilly had come over to help with the preparations for the Fête to be held in three weeks' time, although the advertising posters she had agreed to distribute twisted a knife in her chest every time she read the name of the guest of honour.

She hadn't told her cousin of Rod knowing of her identity all the time, deciding it was better Kathy was left in ignorance of the fact. It would only upset her anew, and there seemed little real point in that.

'I feel fine,' she dismissed, knowing it was sleepless nights that made her look so awful. 'He's still coming then?' she indicated the poster in her hand.

'Hm?' Kathy frowned as she looked up, then nodded as she realised Keilly was talking about Rod. 'He telephoned me a couple of weeks ago to confirm that he was.'

'Oh?'

'I thought it was quite decent of him to do so,' Kathy added grudgingly.

'Very,' she agreed abruptly. 'You never mentioned the call before.'

'You haven't seemed to want to talk about him lately,' her cousin shrugged. 'I didn't think you would be interested.'

Not interested! That had to be the understatement of the year; until this moment she hadn't realised how starved for information about Rod she really was. She had tried to tell herself that a clean break was best, that it was better not to know anything about him, and yet her eagerness to hear about him now told her that for her it wasn't true.

'How did he sound?' she asked casually.

'The same as usual, damned sexy,' Kathy grimaced. 'He was very polite, quite friendly really,' she added thoughtfully.

'Did he—did he ask about—any of us?' She held her breath as she waited for the answer.

'Only generally. I——' she broke off as the telephone began to ring. 'Hello?' she spoke into the receiver, glancing up at Keilly as she received an answer. 'How strange, we were just talking about you. Who is *we*?' she glanced up at Keilly once again. 'Keilly and me,' she answered. 'We were just discussing the Fête. You're still coming, aren't you?' she asked anxiously.

Keilly knew who the caller was, of course, her whole body tensing. She turned to look out of the window, could almost imagine Rod at the other end of the telephone line, tall and strong, and so achingly handsome.

'Keilly?'

She turned with a start as she realised Kathy had been talking to her and she hadn't heard her. 'Mm?' she quirked dark brows.

'Rod called to talk to you,' Kathy held out the receiver.

Keilly stared at it wordlessly, moving forward jerkily as she sensed her cousin was becoming impatient with her. 'Yes?' she spoke breathlessly into the receiver.

For a heart-stopping few moments there was complete silence on the other end of the line. 'Keilly?' Rod finally spoke.

'Yes,' she confirmed huskily.

'I called the hotel first and your aunt told me you were here; I hope you don't mind my telephoning you at your cousin's?'

He sounded so distant, like a stranger and not the man who had made love to her. 'Not at all,' her own voice was as stilted. 'What did you want to talk to me about?'

'The second letter you wrote to the magazine,' he said instantly. 'You didn't have to do it, but I appreciated it.'

She had written to the magazine again just after Rod left Selchurch, telling them how wrong she had been about the film 'Beginning Again', that it was a beautiful and sensitive film, and that Rod played it as such. It had been the least she could do in the circumstances, and the magazine had published the second letter in this month's issue.

'I only wrote the truth,' she told him abruptly.

'Well I appreciated it,' he insisted again. 'How are you, Keilly?'

Was it her imagination or had his voice warmed a little? She decided it must be her imagination, that she wanted it to be that way when it really wasn't. 'I'm well,' she answered curtly. 'And you?'

'Working when I really intended to take a holiday, but otherwise I'm well too.'

'I'm glad,' she ignored the jibe about his holiday. 'Well if that was all . . .?' She was very aware of Kathy listening to her side of the conversation at least, even if he wasn't.

'Keilly!' he sharply stopped her as she would have rung off. 'How are you really?' his voice had lowered huskily, and this time she knew she hadn't imagined it.

'As I said I'm fine,' she replied stiffly.

'You damned little coward!' He rang off abruptly.

She knew the reason for his anger, but she had no intention of questioning Kathy about something that caused her cousin to much pain.

'Is everything all right?' Kathy asked curiously.

'Yes,' she dismissed, turning away from the telephone. 'Now shall we get on with sorting these posters?'

Kathy took the hint not to probe, although she did give Keilly several curious looks. Keilly was aware of them but chose to ignore them, and soon they returned to work as if Rod had never telephoned. As far as Kathy was concerned anyway!

CHAPTER NINE

EVERYTHING looked wonderful for the Fête, the stalls and sideshows all laid out nicely in the extensive grounds of The Hall, the weather holding out for them too, the sun shining brightly, with not a cloud in the sky to mar the day.

There may not be any clouds overhead, but Keilly had several inside her that refused to go away. She was very nervous about facing Rod again, so nervous in fact, that she had invited Michael Fenwick to accompany her this afternoon. She had been out with him several times in the last weeks, mainly to take her mind off Rod more than any real desire to go out with Michael. She wasn't being fair to him, she knew that, but for this afternoon at least she needed the support of his company.

'Well we're all ready.' Kathy came to stand at her side to survey their morning's work. 'Let's just hope the people turn up this afternoon.'

'I think the whole town is coming,' Keilly told her dryly. 'Everyone I've spoken to has said they are.'

'We've got a big drawing attraction this year,' Kathy nodded. 'And I don't mean the Fête!'

'Er—Has Rod arrived yet?' she tried to sound uninterested.

'Not that I know of. Didn't Mum say something about him booking into the hotel?'

'Yes,' she answered abruptly. A woman she presumed to be the capable Barbie had telephoned the hotel the previous week and booked two rooms for overnight in Rod's name. She had been wondering ever since who the second room was for. 'He's bringing someone with him,' she added stiltedly.

'Probably a girlfriend,' Kathy dismissed it as of no importance.

Keilly eyed her curiously. 'Doesn't it bother you? After all, you did think you loved him once.'

Her cousin gave her a glaring look, taking her arm to lead her towards the house. 'I wish you would stop making remarks like that where we can be overhead,' she hissed.

'Sorry,' Keilly grimaced. 'But doesn't it bother you he may be bringing a girlfriend down here?' It certainly bothered her!

'Not in the least,' Kathy dismissed. 'She'll help divert his attention.'

Keilly couldn't view the fact that Rod wasn't coming here alone quite so dispassionately. He must know what it would do to her to see him with another woman, he couldn't be that insensitive, in fact she knew him to be the opposite. Maybe he wanted to hurt her as he claimed she had hurt him.

Whatever the reason, and whoever his guest was, she dressed with special care that afternoon, wearing a dress of turquoise, its silky material clinging to her lovingly, her make-up a little heavier than usual in an effort to cover her pallor and the dark circles beneath her eyes, eyes that somehow seemed to have taken on the colour of her dress. Her hair was dark and gleaming, secured back lightly at her temples with two turquoise combs, her only jewellery the cross and chain about her throat that her mother had given her years ago.

Michael was openly appreciative of her appearance when he called for her at two o'clock, the Fête due to open at two-thirty, Keilly agreeing to get there early in case she had to help out at all.

She froze as she and Michael turned to leave and walked straight into Rod and the woman talking animatedly at his side. They stared at each other for long timeless minutes, both Michael and the beautiful blonde woman fading into the background during that time, their senses attuned only to each other.

Finally it was the blonde woman who broke the tense atmosphere. 'Aren't you going to introduce us, Rod?' she prompted pointedly.

He dragged his gaze away from Keilly with effort, looking at the woman at his side. Keilly followed his gaze, the woman about Rod's own age, possibly a little older—although she knew age wouldn't matter to him if he were genuinely attracted to a woman! She was a tall woman, very slender, very beautiful, and more important, very confident in herself. Keilly felt decidedly inadequate next to her, despite the care she had taken with her own appearance.

'Of course,' Rod spoke smoothly. 'This is Mrs Grant's neice Keilly, and her friend Michael Fenwick. Keilly, Michael, this is my secretary, Barbie Daniels.'

The identity of the other woman didn't seem half as important as the way Rod had chosen to introduce Keilly, as if she had never meant any more to him than being the niece of the owner of the hotel! She looked at him with widely hurt eyes, feeling almost as if he had physically slapped her in the face.

'I'm pleased to meet you both,' Barbie said in a friendly voice, her grey suit and black blouse expertly tailored, a perfect match for the grey suit and black shirt Rod wore.

'And you,' Michael was the one to answer her. 'Are you just on your way to The Hall?'

'That's right,' Rod nodded. 'You?'

'The same,' Michael smiled, picking up none of the

strain between the other man and Keilly.

'I'll just go to the desk and hand in our keys, Rod,' his secretary told him.

The tension was even stronger in Keilly as the other woman walked away to the desk, not having spoken at all since she had turned and seen Rod. His secretary was a little different from what she had imagined she would be, nothing at all like the mother of three children should look.

'Er—It's nice to have seen you again, Rod,' she finally said awkwardly. 'When did you arrive?'

There was nothing to be learnt of his own feelings at seeing her again from his expression, his eyes devoid of emotion, his face bland. 'About an hour ago,' he answered her politely. 'Just time enough to have lunch before we had to leave for The Hall.'

He must have arrived while she had been in her room changing; if only she could have managed to completely avoid such personal encounters! 'We mustn't keep you,' she dismissed. 'Michael and I were just leaving ourselves.'

He nodded distantly, his eyes cold now. 'Perhaps we will see you later.'

'I'm sure you will,' Michael smiled.

Keilly was still shaking when they reached Michael's car, gratefully she got into the passenger seat, not sure how much longer her legs would hold her. It was all so much worse than she had imagined, Rod acting like a stranger to her, his secretary seeming so much more now that she had seen the other woman. Barbie Daniels was beautiful, how could Rod not find her attractive?

'I think I'd like a secretary who looked like that,' Michael unwittingly poured salt on the open wound.

'She is *Mrs* Daniels,' Keilly heard herself defend icily. 'And she has three children.'

'Oh,' Michael looked suitably abashed. 'Still,' he brightened. 'Married or not, she would cheer my office up no end.'

Keilly didn't answer, aware that the other woman would cheer up any man's office 'no end', and any other place she cared to be! She wished they had never spoken to the other couple, wished she had never met Rod at all!

He opened the Fête with all the charm and humour she knew he was capable of, was nothing at all like the coldly grim stranger she had just met at the hotel, the crowds of people who had turned out to see him not disappointed as he charmed every single one of them with the small speech he made before declaring the Fête open.

'Not bad,' Barbie drawled at Keilly's side, having come to stand there without Keilly being aware of it, Michael a short distance away talking to his parents. 'Considering he has never done anything like this before,' she added mockingly.

'But—don't people like him do this sort of thing all the time?' Keilly was curious in spite of herself.

Blue eyes deepened with laughter. 'Not stars of Rod's calibre,' Barbie smiled. 'I had to come here with him just to make sure he wasn't kidding me.'

Keilly flushed her resentment. 'Well I hope we've provided you with a little entertainment——'

'Hey,' the other woman stopped her chidingly. 'Rod warned me you were full of prickles, he wasn't wrong.'

She paled. 'Rod spoke to you about me?'

'Only in passing,' Barbie dismissed. 'And I didn't come up here to laugh at anyone. I just couldn't believe Rod was really going to do this. He was quite good.'

Keilly made no comment to the statement, even though it was the truth. How dare Rod tell this woman about her! And what, exactly, *had* he told her?

Barbie was watching her with narrowed eyes. 'So you're the woman who wrote those letters about Rod,' she mused. 'Strange, you don't look the vindictive type.'

'I'm not,' she flushed.

'No, probably not,' the other woman acknowledged. 'The second letter was certainly a nice gesture. I know Rod was pleased about it. He certainly seemed a lot happier after he had seen it, anyway,' she added thoughtfully.

'Really,' she said uninterestedly.

'The woman in the red dress is your cousin?' Barbie suddenly asked curiously.

Keilly followed her line of vision to where Kathy was in her element as she introduced Rod to the people crowding around him. 'Yes,' she acknowledged dully.

'Attractive,' Barbie drawled.

'Yes,' she agreed flatly.

Barbie turned to look at her. 'But nothing at all like a sea witch,' she murmured.

Keilly raised startled lashes, all colour leaving her face. 'What do you mean?' Her lips felt too stiff to articulate properly. 'Mrs Daniels——'

'Barbie,' the other woman corrected smoothly, 'and you'll have to excuse me, I think I had better go and rescue Rod,' she gave Keilly a preoccupied smile. 'He's likely to get crushed by the masses otherwise!' She began to push her way through the crowd, leaving a dazed Keilly behind her.

That comment by Barbie Daniels about a sea witch had been no accident, so just what had Rod told his secretary about her? She had no opportunity to ask him as he seemed to be surrounded by people for most of the afternoon.

'I went to see his film several weeks ago,' once again

it was Michael who added salt to the wound. 'I thought it was very good.'

'Why don't you go and tell him so?' she snapped. 'I'm sure he would like to hear it!'

Michael gave her a wounded look, not understanding what he had said to upset her. 'Would you like me to go and get you some more lemonade?' he offered to ease the tension.

She hadn't drunk the cup she already had, but she nodded acceptance. 'Thank you, this one is a bit warm,' she handed the cup to him before he went away, the promise of a beautiful day fulfilled with the warm sunshine and a clear blue sky, the fresh lemonade her aunt had provided proving very popular.

In fact the whole Fête was a success, more successful than it had ever been before, and she knew Kathy would be pleased with the amount of money she would have to send to charity, the usual recipient of any money they made. But the afternoon was a disaster as far as Keilly was concerned. Everywhere she looked she seemed to see Rod, a laughing smiling Rod whose eyes glazed over coldly every time their glances happened to meet. He had far from forgiven her for what he considered her lack of faith in him.

It was with relief that she persuaded Michael to take her home shortly before five, although the Fête was still crowded and looked like going on for several more hours yet. She cried off seeing Michael that evening too, her excuse of a headache a real one. The afternoon had been a terrible strain on her, and it was with a sigh of gratitude that she lay down in her darkened bedroom, falling asleep almost instantly.

She felt a strange prickling sensation down her spine as she began to wake up, the curtains no longer necessary to keep out the sunlight, the sky beginning to darken outside. The weird sensation of not being alone persisted as she blinked into wakefulness, and as she looked about the gloom of the room she saw the man seated in the chair beside her bed, sitting there as if he had every right to do so.

'Rod!' she gasped in recognition, sitting up. 'I—What are you doing here?' she demanded, pushing the tangle of her hair out of her eyes. 'My aunt——'

'Told me you were lying down because you don't feel well,' he finished.

'I doubt she expected you to come in here!' she scorned, still trembling from the shock of finding him in her bedroom.

'Probably not,' he acknowledged abruptly. 'But I wanted to talk to you.'

'What about?' she was at once on the defensive. 'Haven't you already talked *about* me enough?'

His eyes narrowed. 'Explain that remark,' he snapped.

She was becoming accustomed to the gloom of her room now, could see him quite clearly, was unperturbed by his grim expression. 'Your secretary seems well informed.'

'I said explain it,' he repeated with abrupt anger.

Keilly became flushed, never having seen him like this before, wondering if it were possible he had suffered as much as she had the last few weeks. 'Mrs Daniels seemed to imply she knew about us, she even called me "sea witch",' she added accusingly.

'Barbie knows nothing about us, Keilly,' he rasped. 'Or if she does it's only what she's surmised from my behaviour. She called you sea witch because when she asked I told her that was what was bothering me. I never once mentioned you by name.'

She blushed her regret at misjudging him. 'I'm sorry,' she mumbled.

'Are you?' his mouth twisted bitterly. 'Are you really? Or do you still think I go around boasting of my conquests to anyone who will listen?'

She paled as suddenly as the colour had entered her cheeks. 'That wasn't what I said,' she gasped. 'You're twisting my words——'

'Have you spoken to Kathy?' he interrupted icily.

She swallowed hard. 'I speak to her all the time——'

'That isn't what *I* meant, and you know it,' he stood up impatiently, changed into close-fitting denims and a casual shirt. 'Damn it, Keilly, why won't you believe me?' he groaned. 'Do you have any idea how much I've missed you the last nine weeks? How much I've longed for you?'

'You knew where to find me,' she muttered.

'And you know damn well I can't live with your distrust!'

'I'm sorry,' she looked down at her hands.

Rod's eyes glittered with his fury as he wrenched her chin up. 'You aren't sorry at all, if you were you would want to know the truth. Damn it, you would *demand* it.'

She trembled at the fire in his eyes. 'I—I can't,' she choked.

'You mean you're frightened to,' he pushed her away from him with disgust. 'You're talking about your cousin's pride; I'm talking about our whole lives together. It's obvious which means more to you!' He slammed out of the room.

And Keilly knew that he had finally slammed out of her life, that he would never ask for her understanding again. God, what was she to do, what *could* she do? To go to Kathy and accuse her of lying was unthinkable, to watch Rod walk out of her life again, this time for good, was unbearable!

'Rod's gone,' Barbie Daniels told her the next morning when she asked for him.

'Gone?' she frowned her puzzlement. 'Gone where?'

The blonde woman shrugged. 'He decided to go to California early; he left last night.'

'Without you?'

'Without me,' Barbie nodded. 'He flew back, I'm taking the car.'

'I see,' she chewed on her bottom lip.

'I wish I did!' Barbie sighed, taking sympathy on her. 'He didn't say much to me, just that he was leaving, but I take it he spoke to you some time before he left?'

'Yes,' she admitted raggedly, wondering what she was going to do now. She needed to talk to Rod.

'I don't know what the problem is between you two,' the other woman watched her with narrowed eyes. 'But I do know that Rod has been acting like a man who just lost his best friend—or the woman he loves? Am I right?'

'I——'

'Do you love him, Keilly?'

'Yes,' she answered truthfully. 'I love him very much.'

'Then I don't see what the problem is?' Barbie frowned her confusion.

'You wouldn't understand,' she avoided the other woman's probing gaze. 'It's too complicated.'

'Try me,' she invited softly.

'No. I——'

'Keilly, Rod has never been a man to give up on something he wants,' Barbie cut in impatiently. 'Which means the problem lies with you. So what is it if you love him too? Maybe I can help you,' she encouraged.

'I don't think so,' she shook her head. 'Do you have any idea when he'll be back in England?'

'About a week, I should think,' the other woman frowned. 'Do you intend seeing him then?'

'Yes,' she answered firmly. 'I—I have to talk to him. I have to explain——'

'Why wait until he comes back if it's that important?' Barbie prompted. 'Why not talk to him now?'

'You said he's gone to America . . .'

'So?'

She gave a nervous laugh. 'You aren't suggesting I follow him there?'

'And if I am?'

'Mrs Daniels, being Rod's secretary you may have become used to jetting all over the world, but people like me do not just up and leave for America. Especially when they're unsure of their welcome,' she added worriedly. She had decided during the long night that she had to trust Rod, had to believe whatever he told her. Because she had no life without him.

'Keilly, I——' Barbie broke off, looking over Keilly's shoulder. 'If I'm not mistaken,' she said slowly. 'Your cousin looks and feels as bad as you do.'

She turned sharply to look at Kathy, shocked by how pale she was. 'Is there anything wrong?' she demanded anxiously. 'Peter . . .? Heather . . .?'

'They're both fine,' Kathy dismissed, glancing uncomfortably at Barbie. 'I need to talk to you, Keilly. Alone,' she added awkwardly.

'Don't worry about me,' Barbie said goodnaturedly. 'I was just going in to breakfast anyway. I'll see you later, Keilly,' she added softly, reminding Keilly their conversation was far from over.

'Can we go up to your bedroom?' Kathy asked once they were alone. 'I don't want to be overheard.'

Keilly couldn't imagine what on earth was wrong with her cousin, but as she looked so anxious she took her straight up to her bedroom. 'What's wrong?' she asked again once the door was closed. 'Kathy, tell me what's happened!' she pleaded.

Her cousin was very pale, her eyes deep brown pools. She sat down heavily on the bedroom chair. 'I had a telephone call from Rod late last night,' she revealed dully.

All the colour drained from Keilly's face, leaving her as pale as Kathy. 'Oh no,' she groaned, knowing he had taken things into his own hands and spoken to Kathy himself.

Kathy looked up at her with tortured eyes. 'I had no idea—Maybe I just didn't want to see——' She bit down hard on her bottom lip. 'I didn't want to admit to myself that you and Rod were in love,' she explained raggedly. 'Because if I had done that it would have changed everything.'

'Kathy,' she came down on the carpet in front of her cousin. 'Kathy, what did Rod tell you?'

'Only what I already knew, subconsciously,' she choked. 'That the two of you were in love, and that I was keeping you apart.'

'He said that?' she gasped at his cruelty.

'Not the last bit,' Kathy gave her a wan smile. 'He's too much of a gentleman to accuse me of that! He telephoned to say goodbye, he said,' she recalled woodenly, 'that he doubted he would ever come back to Selchurch again. That even though he loved you, and believed you loved him, that something more important was keeping you apart.' She looked at Keilly with shadowed eyes, 'It's me, isn't it?' she urged.

'Kathy——'

'Isn't it?' she persisted.

Keilly stood up. 'Rod had no right to call you, to upset you in this way——'

'He had every right,' her cousin said flatly. 'He's fighting for what he wants.'

'But at your expense!'

Kathy sighed. 'He's known all along who I was, hasn't he?'

She looked at her cousin with pained eyes. 'Yes.'

'I thought so,' she nodded, smiling sadly. 'He hasn't changed at all, he's still protective. Even after I lied to him to get him to take me to bed he didn't blame me, was more concerned that he may have hurt me. And I felt so humiliated,' her voice broke. 'So deceitful!'

Keilly frowned, shaking her head. 'After *you* lied?' she repeated. 'But I thought——'

'Oh, Keilly, surely you've guessed the truth by now?' Kathy groaned guiltily. 'Rod didn't seduce *me*. I knew he found me attractive, so I encouraged him shamelessly, told him I was experienced, that he had nothing to worry about. It took him half an hour to recover from the shock when he realised the truth!'

As she lay thinking about it last night Keilly had guessed it had to be something like this, had known Rod would never lie to her, that he had never deliberately hurt anyone. But to hear Kathy admitting it still stunned her . . .!

'He was so worried about me,' Kathy remembered abruptly. 'Told me how stupid I had been to lie as I had, that I was the type of girl who would one day regret it bitterly. God, did I regret it!' she moaned.

'Was that why you lied to me on your wedding day?'

She nodded, looking down at her hands. 'That one time with Rod, it was the only time I was stupid enough to——' she bit her lip painfully. 'Well, as he predicted, I regretted it. By my wedding day my guilt was eating me up and I had to talk to someone about it. I chose you to burden with it. Pride made me say it was Rod's fault. You've always been like my little sister, Keilly, and I knew how you would feel about me if I told you the truth.' She gave a wan smile. 'You've championed me wonderfully, Keilly,' she said huskily. 'But I can't let you sacrifice your chance of happiness because of me. I told Peter everything last night——'

'Oh no,' she groaned.

Kathy nodded. 'He's known all along that there was someone before him, but he considered it was my business if I didn't want to talk about it.' Tears shimmered in her eyes. 'I seem to have been protected all my life by one person or another, it's time I stopped hiding behind lies to save my pride. Peter has been—wonderful about this, as I should have realised he would be. I wish now that I had taken your advice on my wedding day, Keilly, and spoken to Peter then. Perhaps if I had none of this would have happened.'

She didn't know what to say, couldn't think what words of comfort would help her cousin now.

'I haven't been afraid of Rod recognising me,' Kathy continued softly. 'I was more afraid he would remember what had really happened and tell you the truth.'

She shook her head. 'He wouldn't do that.'

'No,' Kathy acknowledged. 'I should have known that he wouldn't, not even if it meant losing you. It was just that I had lived with the lie so long I couldn't bear for the truth to come out. I've been a coward, but no longer.'

'You know that this will never go any further, don't you?' Keilly prompted softly. 'It was all a long time ago, I think it's better if it's forgotten.'

The tears began to fall unchecked down Kathy's pale cheeks. 'I think I've known all along that Rod would never tell anyone what really happened, known he was too much of a gentleman to reveal how stupid I had been. I just couldn't be sure.'

'You can now,' Keilly said with certainty.

'Yes,' Kathy sighed. 'But at what cost? Is it too late for the two of you to work things out?'

She turned away. 'Rod's gone.'

'Gone?' Kathy looked startled. 'What do you mean, he's gone? I only spoke to him last night——'

'Wherever he telephoned you from it wasn't here,' Keilly told her. 'Barbie said he left soon after he had spoken to me, which was quite early.'

'But I——' Kathy was very pale again. 'After all this I'm too late, aren't I?'

She sighed. 'I don't know. Maybe not,' she comforted as her cousin looked stricken.

'If he's in London can't you——'

'He isn't,' she said dully. 'He flew to America today.'

'Oh,' Kathy sighed.

'Look, you go on home now,' she decided firmly. 'I have some thinking to do, and I'm sure you would like to get back to Peter. Everything really is all right between the two of you?' she probed worriedly.

Kathy's smile was dazzling with happiness. 'It's better than it's ever been, because there are no secrets between us now.'

Keilly could understand that, there had been too many secrets between herself and Rod. But last night after he had gone she had realised he had to be protecting Kathy in some way, had even half guessed in what way it was. Poor Kathy, to have lived with that lie all these years. And poor Rod, to have been blamed, accused, of something he hadn't done.

But it warmed her, gave her hope, that even after he had left her last night, supposedly for the last time, he had made one last desperate attempt for their happiness, had telephoned Kathy in the hope that she would realise how important it was that she told the truth.

But what should she do now? Should she follow him to America, perhaps risk being rejected for her lack of faith in him? Or should she play it safe and stay here, wait until he returned to London and then contact him? It would be a long week if she did the latter.

CHAPTER TEN

As she sat on the plane the next day waiting to take off for Los Angeles she understood Rod's complete dependence on Barbie when it came to organisation. The other woman had lost no time in booking her flight the previous day, had helped her pack, and had even driven her down to London in Rod's car.

Keilly had decided to tell Rod's secretary of her decision shortly after Kathy left, had found the other woman just leaving the dining room. 'Could I talk to you?' she requested huskily.

'Of course,' Barbie agreed instantly. 'Would you like to go somewhere more private?' she grimaced as people from the dining room began to push past them, the hotel filled almost to capacity this holiday weekend.

'I think that might be a good idea,' she nodded ruefully.

'How about my room?' the other woman arched blonde brows.

'All right.' She followed Barbie up the stairs to her room, a very orderly room, even the bed made, although Keilly knew the cleaning ladies wouldn't have got this far just yet.

Barbie smiled at her revealing expression. 'I always do it,' she laughed softly. 'I think it's a throwback from having to be so organised at home; sometimes there I start to make the bed before my husband has got out of it! It isn't always easy juggling my career with my family, although ultimately my husband and children come first. Rod knows and accepts that,' she sat down on the meticulously made bed.

Her own humour faded at the mention of Rod. 'I've decided to—to go to America,' she told the other woman in a rush—before she had time to change her mind!

'Good for you,' Barbie said approvingly.

Keilly reserved judgment on the sense of what she was doing until she had seen and spoken to Rod. 'What I need to know from you is where Rod is staying. And also——'

'Now don't worry about a thing,' Barbie cut in firmly. 'I'll arrange it all.'

'But——'

'Just relax, Keilly,' she advised as she lifted up the telephone receiver and began to dial. 'I'm used to doing this sort of thing.'

'What sort of thing?' she asked in a panicked voice, listening incredulously as Barbie was apparently connected with an airline, making arrangements for a seat for Keilly on tomorrow's flight. 'I can't afford first class!' she squeaked as Barbie put the telephone down with a satisfied smile. 'I was thinking more in the Economy class,' she did a mental calculation of her savings. 'Or crawling in with the baggage,' she added lamely.

'Don't be silly,' Barbie dismissed such an idea. 'Rod always travels first class, and he would be very angry with me if I let you go to him any other way. Just relax, Keilly,' she repeated soothingly. 'If you're going to be Rod's wife you'll have to get used to this sort of treatment.'

Dull colour darkened her cheeks. 'We haven't discussed marriage——'

'You will,' the other woman predicted with certainty.

Keilly wasn't so sure, but she didn't particularly care one way or the other. She wanted to be with Rod, and although he had told her he loved her and implied they would have a long relationship, he had never mentioned marriage. She no longer cared about such things, just wanted to be with him for as long as he needed her.

'Now you go and start packing,' Barbie instructed. 'I'll be up to help you as soon as I've booked your hotel room.'

'My air-ticket——'

'We'll pick that up tomorrow when we get to the airport. Please just leave all the details to me, Keilly,' she chided mockingly. 'It's my job, remember?'

She felt suitably chastened, learning over the next twenty-four hours that Barbie was very good at her job. She had driven her to the airport with plenty of time to pick up the ticket and see that she was shown to the first-class lounge after booking in. After that Keilly had been taken over by the airline staff, taken to the flight gate, personally seated, her every wish granted during the hours of the flight. Her only previous experience of flying had been a school-trip six years ago, but then it had been a chartered flight, certainly nothing like this preferential treatment, although she had an idea some of it was due to Barbie's whispered instructions when she took her to the desk to book in.

As they neared Los Angeles she felt her stomach begin to do somersaults, going over Barbie's instructions for when she landed for the hundredth time. Just tell the taxi driver the name of her hotel and he will do the rest, the name of her hotel was written on the piece of paper in her jacket pocket. It sounded simple enough; she only hoped it proved to be that way!

All thought of the taxi and getting to the hotel fled her mind as she saw the man waiting for her at the airport. She walked towards Rod as if in a trance, not caring how he came to be here to meet her, only knowing she was glad that he was.

Her heart felt as if it would burst with happiness by the time she reached his open arms, launching herself against him, laughing and crying at the same time, touching him as if she never wanted to stop, all misunderstandings fleeing as their mouths met in fiery passion.

'I'd love to stand here like this all day,' Rod finally broke the kiss to murmur against her temple, holding her tightly as she couldn't seem to stop shaking. 'But we're causing rather a congestion!' he added teasingly.

For the first time she became conscious of the fellow-travellers who were trying to get past them as they partly blocked their exit. Her blush at their curious looks soon became painfully obvious.

Rod laughed indulgently. 'They're used to this sort of thing at airports.'

'I'm not,' she burrowed against his shirtfront to hide her embarrassment.

'Let's get out of here,' he growled.

She was quite willing to do that, allowing him to take her luggage as he led the way to a long black limousine waiting outside. 'Yours?' she asked softly as the driver quickly got out of the car to help put the luggage in the boot.

'Courtesy of the people who organise the Oscars,' he told her ruefully as he climbed into the back of the car beside her. 'When they realise I haven't even turned up for the presentation I doubt they will be feeling so friendly,' he grimaced, his arm about her shoulders as he held her to his side. 'But enough about that. Tell me——'

'Rod, what do you mean you haven't turned up?' she sat back to look at him. 'I'm sure you're going to win.'

'Maybe I will,' he shrugged, very lean and attractive in fitted denims and a blue short-sleeved shirt. 'If I do I've arranged for someone else to go up and collect it.'

Keilly's eyes widened. 'You make it sound as if you win Oscars every day!'

'On the contrary,' he smiled at her. 'I've never won one.'

'Then why did you miss the chance to collect this one?' she demanded indignantly. 'When I asked you about it before you told me you were polite enough just to attend if you were nominated, that it didn't matter if you won or not. You——'

'Keilly, when Barbie telephoned me yesterday and told me you were coming here today, and what time you were arriving, I had to make a choice, whether to meet you or go to the Oscars. There really was no choice,' the loving expression in his eyes told her she would always come first with him.

She swallowed hard, not knowing whether to stay angry with him or kiss him. The latter won. 'I love you. I love you, Rod,' she murmured between kisses, oblivious to the fact that they weren't alone. 'But I insist you go to the Oscars. Is it too late?' she asked anxiously.

'No, people will only just be arriving now. But——'

'Then you're to go,' she decided firmly. 'We can talk when you get back.'

'I'm not going anywhere without you,' he told her equally as stubbornly.

'You have to——'

'No.'

She sighed at his implacability. 'I'll be quite happy waiting for you at the hotel.'

'If I go you go.' He looked at her challengingly.

She gave a start of surprise. 'I'm not invited. I'm not

completely naïve, Rod, you have to be invited to these sort of things months ahead.'

He shook his head. 'My invitation said it was for myself and a guest.'

'Oh.'

'So what's it to be?' he arched dark brows. 'Do we both go or neither of us?'

As she looked into the warm love of his eyes she felt the last fears and doubts leave her. 'We both go,' she told him determinedly. 'But we have so much to talk about, Rod. I have so much to tell you. Kathy came to see me, and——'

'We can discuss it all later,' he hugged her tightly to him. 'All that matters at the moment is that you're here and we're together.'

For the moment it did seem to be enough, the drive to the hotel passing all too quickly for Keilly, Rod's kisses reducing her to a quivering mass of desire.

'I'll take you swimming tomorrow,' he promised her as they drove by the ocean.

She looked at the stillness of the deep blue water. 'It doesn't look very challenging,' she derided.

'No?' he mocked, dark brows raised. 'But I shall be with you,' he added pointedly.

She gave a husky laugh of pure enjoyment. 'In that case I've changed my mind; it would be the biggest challenge of my life!'

Rod wasted no time going to the desk to book her in once they reached the hotel, striding across the lobby to the lift with her at his side, the hotel seeming curiously empty after the rush and bustle of the city outside. 'Most of the people staying here have gone to the theatre for the Oscars,' he explained as they went up in the almost silent lift.

Her eyes widened. 'You mean I could bump into

people like Glenda Jackson or Lauren Bacall, or Richard Gere, or——'

He laughed indulgently, shaking his head. 'A lot of the people invited actually live near here, at Malibu or Bel Air. I'll take you for a drive round tomorrow,' he told her at her awestruck expression. 'Point out all the places of interest.'

She blushed as they stepped out into the carpeted hallway, allowing him to lead the way to her room. 'I must seem very silly to you,' she mumbled. 'Oh, Rod, I'm afraid I'm going to embarrass you—Goodness,' she gasped as they entered the huge suite, the masculine articles lying about the lounge showing signs of habitation. 'This is beautiful,' she breathed, 'but I can't stay here. Barbie promised me she would——'

'Barbie knows I wouldn't let you stay anywhere else but with me in my suite,' he cut in softly.

She swallowed hard as his words penetrated, moistening her lips with the tip of her pink tongue. 'Your—suite?' she repeated slowly.

'Yes,' his mouth tightened slightly. 'And this will be your bedroom,' he opened the door to the right of the lounge.

She glanced inside, finding it was as glamorous as the room they were in now, although its tidyness showed none of the habitation of the other room. 'Which room do you sleep in?' she asked shyly.

He shrugged. 'Over here,' he opened a door on the other side of the lounge, revealing a bedroom much like the one she had just looked at, except this one obviously showed signs of Rod's presence, his brush and cufflinks on the dressing-table, a towel thrown over a chair from where he had recently taken a shower, a discarded newspaper on the bed.

She strolled past him, looking about her appreciatively. 'I think I prefer this room.'

'They're identical,' he said dryly.

She looked at him with unflinching grey eyes. 'No, they aren't,' she shook her head. 'You sleep in this one too.'

'Keilly——' he was interrupted by the soft knock sounding on the outer door. 'That will be your luggage,' he predicted.

'Oh good,' she turned to follow him from the room. 'You can help me decide what to wear,' she frowned. 'I don't think I packed anything suitable . . .'

Rod gave her an exasperated look before letting in the porter with her bags. 'I'm really not that interested in going,' he drawled. 'So don't get yourself in a state about it.'

'You *are* going,' she told him firmly after directing the porter to put her suitcase and overnight bag on Rod's bed before he left—*their* bed, she mentally corrected herself, already imagining them together there later. She could hardly wait. 'I was only—Oh, Barbie, you thought of everything,' she spoke softly as she opened her suitcase to find the shimmering grey-blue gown she had worn the night of her aunt and uncle's dinner party. She hadn't packed it, which meant the other woman must have done. 'She really is wonderful,' she told Rod as she shook the gown from its folds in the suitcase, knowing from experience that it wasn't the sort of gown that creased. It hadn't.

He nodded. 'Yes, she is. Although not as wonderful as you.'

She blushed at the compliment. 'Shouldn't you be changing too?' she prompted as she began to undress, slightly unnerved about doing so in front of Rod in the clear light of day, telling herself not to be ridiculous, that he had seen her naked before. Somehow it didn't help.

'Yes,' he turned away, understanding her confusion. 'Feel free to use the shower,' he invited as he began to pull off his shirt. 'I had one before I left for the airport.'

She was grateful for his thoughtfulness, using the shower as an excuse to finish her undressing in the bathroom. It felt a little strange to be putting on evening clothes when it was still light and sunny outside, but she hurriedly showered and changed, determined Rod was going to be at the theatre if—*when* his name was read out for Best Actor.

He looked magnificent when she emerged from the bathroom a few minutes later, very distinguished in the black evening suit and snowy white shirt, his dark hair neatly brushed in place.

'You look beautiful,' he took her in his arms and began kissing her, the caress rapidly deepening to a desperate devouring as he parted her lips with his, engaging in a duel with her tongue that took her breath away. 'Are you sure you wouldn't rather stay here?' he invited huskily. 'You must be tired, wouldn't you rather we—went to bed?'

It was very tempting, longing for the reassurance of his full possession. 'I'd much rather stay here,' she admitted throatily. 'But I want you to be given what is rightly yours.'

He grimaced. 'Even if I'm so nervous I'm shaking with it?'

She moved back a little to look at him, noticing for the first time the white ring of tension about his mouth, the restless movements of his hands. He really was nervous, the man she had believed to have supreme self-confidence at all times. 'Don't worry, darling, I'll be with you,' she gently caressed his rigidly clenched jaw.

'And that's another thing,' he rasped. 'You do realise that today of all days you'll be stared at, wondered about, guessed about, that everyone will be curious to know who you are?'

'It's all right, Rod,' she teased him. 'I don't mind being seen with you if you don't mind being seen with me!'

'You're deliberately misunderstanding me,' he shook her slightly, angry now. 'I'm trying to point out to you that compared to that evening in the restaurant that you hated so much this is going to be a circus.'

'Do you love me?'

'You know I do,' he bit out.

'Then I'll get through this,' she smiled. 'I can do anything if I know you love me.'

'It wasn't enough before.'

'I didn't know you loved me then,' she reminded gently.

'But you know and believe it now?'

'I know and believe it now,' she nodded. 'And I refuse to be diverted. Is the car still waiting downstairs?'

He smiled. 'Probably. Keilly, I've never been so nervous in my life,' he admitted with a groan. 'Today has been the most tense day of my life, the Oscars, and waiting to see if you would get off that plane. Even though Barbie had telephoned me and assured me you were on it I still couldn't believe it would happen.'

'Did you think I had got off half way?' she teased him, her eyes glowing with mischief.

Her levity had the desired effect as he began to smiled. 'With you one can never be sure,' he derided.

'Be sure,' she nodded. 'Now, let's go,' she said forcefully. 'Before they give our seats to someone else.'

'Now that's a thought,' he murmured as he allowed

himself to be dragged out to the lift. 'What will you do then?'

'Stand at the back,' she answered promptly.

'Do they allow that sort of thing at the Oscar ceremonies?' he taunted.

'They do now,' she decided.

There were crowds of people lining the street outside the famous Chinese Theatre, eager fans all trying to get a look at their favourite star. Keilly felt her stomach somersault as the interest in the crowd rose to fever pitch as Rod's many fans began to recognise him. As they stepped out of the car the cheer went up, people of all ages calling for Rod. Whatever nervousness he had betrayed earlier he hid it well now, smiling and waving to the crowd as he guided Keilly into the theatre, seeming unaware of the speculation that suddenly seemed rife.

For Keilly walking through that crowd of people had been an experience she would never forget, the love and admiration that had emanated towards Rod enveloping her too.

After that the whole evening became a magical experience, the audience a glitter of showbusiness entertainers, Rod familiar with most if not all of them, the friendliness once again extended to Keilly as his guest for the evening. She received smiles of acknowledgment from people who had only ever been big names to her, knew that no matter where else she went with Rod she would never forget the excitement and newness of this night.

Rod's hand tightened about hers as the nominees for Best Actor were read out, and when Keilly heard his competition she could understand his tension. Compared to a lot of them his ten years' experience made him a newcomer!

His smile seemed fixed to his lips as the television camera picked him up in the audience. 'If they should happen to say my name,' he told her stiffly. 'And I don't stand up, just kick me!'

She smiled, squeezing his hand reassuringly, although she felt as tense as he did. But she didn't have to kick him as his name was read out, received his excited kiss on the lips with surprised pleasure, her clapping as enthusiastic as everyone else's as he went up to receive the award. She expected him to thank his fellow actors and the people who had worked with him on the film as most of the other lucky winners had done. Instead he stunned her by saying something else completely.

'This is the best wedding present I could have received—besides my lovely fiancée, of course,' he grinned. 'Thank you.'

It was an abrupt, and some would say gratifyingly short speech, compared to some of the lengthy ones that had gone before him, and yet it had much more impact than anything anyone else had said.

Keilly's smile was fixed on her lips as the cameras and audience all focused on her. And no wonder. She had had no warning of what Rod was going to say, was as surprised as everyone else by his announcement. Marriage was something she hadn't dared hope for, just being with him would have been enough.

'I have you trapped now,' he murmured as he took his seat beside her, the attention now turning from them to the next award. 'If you don't marry me now everyone will know you jilted me.'

'Who said anything about not marrying you?' she arched dark brows.

'You mean you will?' his eyes glowed.

'After that announcement I'd be a fool not to,' her gaze was fixed demurely on the stage.

His hand tightened on hers. 'Let's leave,' he grated.

Her mouth quirked. 'You can't take your Oscar and run!' she reproved with amusement.

'Why can't I?' he growled.

'Because, Mr Roderick Richard Bartlett, *I* say you can't!'

He relaxed back with a grin. 'Going to be a bossy wife, are you?' he mused.

'When I get the chance,' she smiled.

'That won't be very often,' he predictably murmured into her ear before sitting silently at her side to watch the rest of the awards.

'We could have one to the party, if you had wanted to,' she told him sleepily a couple of hours later, her head against his bare chest, the two of them back in the hotel suite now, curled up together in bed in the afterglow of their lovemaking. 'I wasn't too tired,' she assured him.

'It must be obvious by the way I rushed you back here that I wasn't interested in the party! I had much more interesting plans in mind,' he added mockingly.

His chest rumbled beneath her ear as he spoke, her fingers idly caressing the dark hair on his chest. 'Yes, calling my aunt and uncle was more interesting,' she taunted him. They had talked to her aunt and uncle for half an hour when they got back to the hotel, Kathy and Peter there too to add their congratulations.

'Witch!' he laughed softly.

'It was nice of you to call them,' she said on a more serious note. 'I know they were a little worried when I decided to rush off after you.'

'And now they are going to have the wedding all organised for when we get back,' his arms tightened about her.

Keilly lifted her head to look at him uncertainly. 'If you want to leave it for a while I'll understand. It was an emotional moment for you when you accepted the Oscar, you can be forgiven for saying things you didn't mean——'

'I meant every word, Keilly,' he interrupted firmly. 'I would have asked you to marry me long ago if I could have cleared up the misunderstanding between us. But for quite a while I didn't even know what it was!'

'I'm sorry I didn't believe in you when you wanted me to,' she mumbled.

'Kathy is your cousin, as close as any sister would have been, of course you had to believe her.'

'But I was coming to you before Kathy told me the truth,' she told him quickly. 'I had decided you couldn't have done the things she accused you of.'

'I know,' he said gently. 'Barbie told me about you coming here,' he explained at her questioning look.

Keilly snuggled against him. 'She really is a very nice person. Do you think she and her husband would like to be godparents to *our* child?'

'You're planning our family already?' Rod teased.

She gave him a mocking look. 'It may have escaped your notice, Mr Bartlett, but you certainly haven't acted like a responsible lover tonight. We could already have started that family, completely *un*planned, I might add.'

For a moment he looked stunned, then his eyes darkened to an appreciative glow. 'Maybe we should just make sure of that fact . . . If you aren't too tired, of course?'

She turned eagerly into his arms. 'I'm never too tired for you. I never will be.'

They could talk more tomorrow, when they didn't need the reassurance of their physical love quite so badly, and then she would tell him about her mother and father. And together they could plan the wonderful life they were going to have together. Yes, tomorrow would be an exciting day. But nowhere near as exciting as here and now, in Rod's arms, being loved by him.

Harlequin Announces...

Harlequin Superromance™

NEW

IMPROVED EXCELLENCE

NSUP-A-1

Beginning with February releases (titles #150 to #153) each of the four Harlequin Superromances will be 308 pages long and have a regular retail price of $2.75 ($2.95 in Canada).

The new shortened Harlequin Superromance guarantees a faster-paced story filled with the same emotional intensity, character depth and plot complexity you have come to expect from Harlequin Superromance.

The tighter format will heighten drama and excitement, and that, combined with a strong well-written romance, will allow you to become more involved with the story from start to finish.

WATCH FOR A SPECIAL INTRODUCTORY PRICE ON HARLEQUIN SUPERROMANCE TITLES #150-#153 IN FEBRUARY

Available wherever paperback books are sold or through Harlequin Reader Service:

In the U.S.
P.O. Box 52040
Phoenix, AZ 85072-2040

In Canada
P.O. Box 2800, Postal Station A
5170 Yonge Street
Willowdale, Ontario M2N 6J3